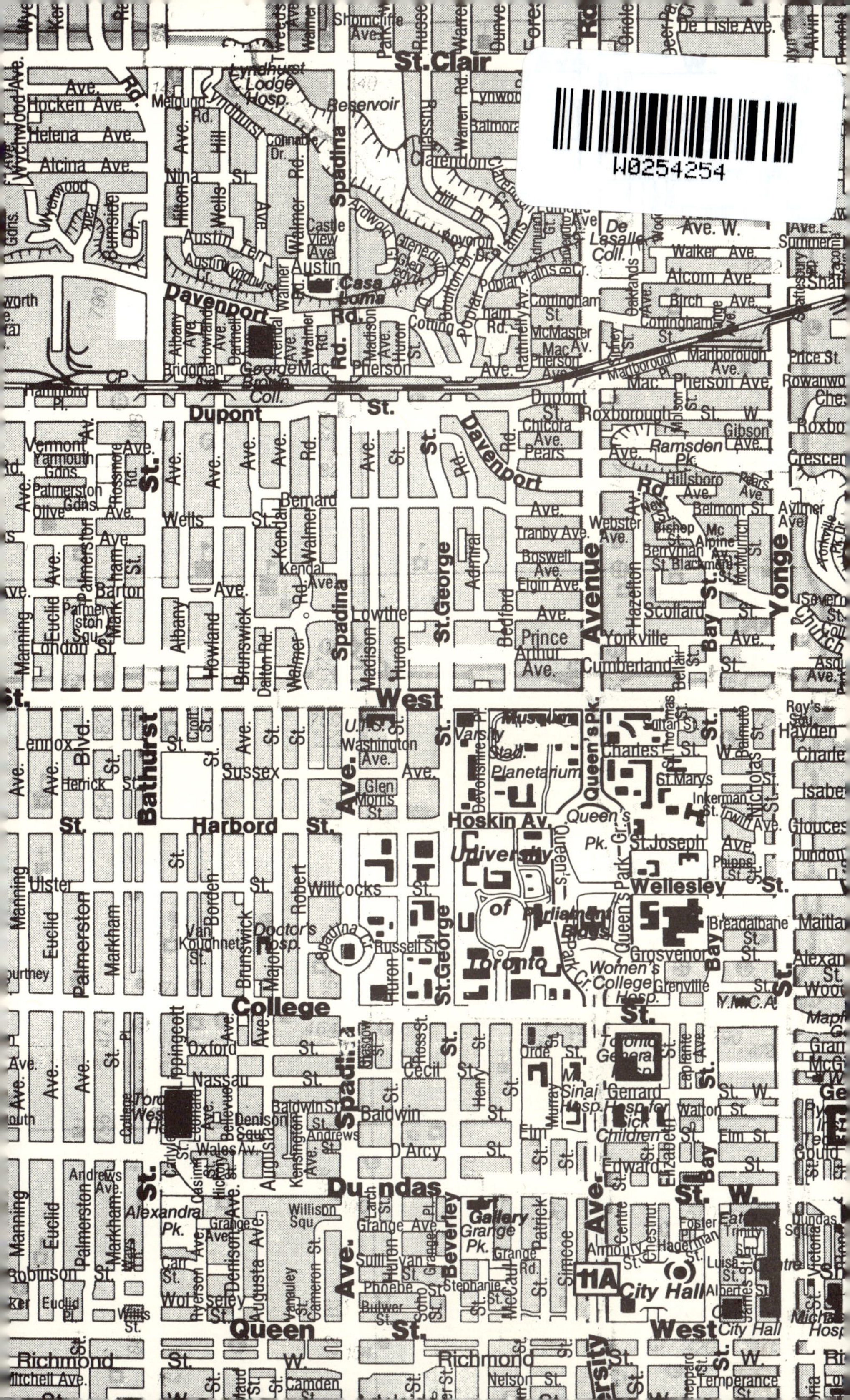
St. Clair
De Lisle Ave.
Lyndhurst Lodge Hosp.
Reservoir
Hocken Ave.
Helena Ave.
Alcina Ave.
Wychwood Ave.
Burnside Dr.
Nina St.
Hilton Ave.
Wells Hill
Walmer Rd.
Spadina
Castle View Ave.
Austin Terr.
Casa Loma
Davenport Rd.
Bridgman Ave.
George Brown Coll.
Madison Ave.
Huron St.
MacPherson Ave.
Poplar Plains Rd.
Cottingham St.
McMaster Av.
De Lasalle Coll.
Oaklands Ave.
Walker Ave.
Alcorn Ave.
Birch Ave.
Cottingham St.
Marlborough Ave.
MacPherson Ave.
Price St.
Summerhill
Shaftesbury
Dupont St.
Roxborough St. W.
Gibson Ave.
Ramsden Pk.
Davenport Rd.
Chicora Ave.
Pears Ave.
Hillsboro Ave.
Belmont St.
Aylmer Ave.
Yorkville
Vermont Ave.
Yarmouth Gdns.
Palmerston Gdns.
Olive Ave.
Bathurst St.
Wells St.
Bernard Ave.
Kendal Ave.
Admiral Rd.
St. George
Bedford Rd.
Tranby Ave.
Boswell Ave.
Elgin Ave.
Webster Ave.
Avenue Rd.
Hazelton Ave.
Bishop
McAlpine St.
Berryman St.
Blackmore St.
McMurrich St.
Yonge
Bay St.
Scollard St.
Yorkville Ave.
Cumberland St.
Prince Arthur Ave.
Lowther
Palmerston Squ.
Barton Ave.
Markham St.
Euclid Ave.
Manning Ave.
London St.
Albany Ave.
Howland Ave.
Brunswick Ave.
Dalton Rd.
Walmer Rd.
Spadina
Madison
Huron
Church St.
Bloor St. West
Lennox
Bathurst
Croft St.
Sussex
U.T.S.
Washington Ave.
Glen Morris St.
Museum
Varsity Stad.
Planetarium
Queen's Pk.
Charles St. W.
St. Thomas St.
Sultan St.
St. Marys
Inkerman St.
Irwin Ave.
Nicholas St.
Hayden
Charles
Isabella
Gloucester
Dundonald
Harbord St.
Hoskin Av.
University of Toronto
Queen's Pk. Cr.
St. Joseph
Phipps
Wellesley St.
Ulster
Willcocks St.
Robert St.
Spadina Cr.
Russell St.
Van Koughnet
Doctor's Hosp.
Major St.
Borden St.
Brunswick
Parliament Bldgs.
Breadalbane St.
Maitland
Grosvenor St.
Alexander St.
Women's College Hosp.
Grenville St.
Y.M.C.A.
Wood
Manning
Euclid
Palmerston
Markham
College
Lippincott
Oxford
Nassau
Glasgow St.
Ross St.
Cecil St.
Henry St.
Orde St.
Murray St.
Mt. Sinai Hosp.
Toronto General
Laplante Ave.
Gerrard St. W.
Hosp. for Sick Children
Walton St.
Elm St.
Gould
Denison Squ.
Baldwin St.
Andrews
Bellevue Ave.
Kensington Ave.
Augusta
D'Arcy
Wales Av.
Toronto Western Hosp.
Edward
Elizabeth St.
Bay St.
Dundas St. W.
Andrews Ave.
Alexandra Pk.
Grange Ave.
Willison Squ.
Larch St.
Beverley St.
Gallery Grange Pk.
Patrick St.
Simcoe
University Ave.
Centre Ave.
Chestnut St.
Armoury
Foster Pl.
Hagerman
Eaton Centre
Trinity Squ.
Dundas Squ.
Victoria
Sullivan St.
Grange Rd.
Stephanie
McCaul St.
Phoebe St.
Soho St.
Bulwer St.
Robinson St.
Wolseley St.
Vanauley
Cameron St.
Ryerson Ave.
Denison Ave.
Willis St.
Queen St.
11A
City Hall
Albert St.
James St.
St. Michael's Hosp.
Queen West
Richmond St. W.
Nelson St.
Mitchell Ave.
Camden
Temperance

blue
bluer
bloor

the martyrology

‘In so moche that in my dayes happened that certayn marchauntes were in a shippe in tamyse, for to have scyled over the sea into zelande, and for lack of wynde, thei taryed atte forlond, and wente to lande for to refreshe them. And one of theym named Sheffelde, a mercer, came in-to an hows and axed for mete, and specyally he axed after egges. And the goode wyf answerede that she could speke no frenshe. And the marchaunt was angry for he also coude speke no frenshe, but wolde have hadde egges, and she understode hym not. And thenne at laste a nother sayd that he wold have eyren. Then the good wyf sayd that she understood him wel. Loo, what sholde a man in thyse days now wryte, egges or eyren. Certaynly it is harde to playse every man be cause of dyversite & chaunge in langage.’

WILLIAM CAXTON

‘The greatest literary masterpiece is no more than an alphabet in disorder.’

JEAN COCTEAU

the martyrology
book 5

bp nichol

The Coach House Press Toronto

Published with the assistance of the Canada Council and the Ontario Arts Council.

ISBN 0-88910-251-1

dear bp

Thank you for your note. It came in the mail on the same day D. Barbour was showing *Sons of Captain Poetry,* so I went and saw it, really excellent. It was weird seeing it, a flash of the past: naturally I recognized the various bit players – Stuart and Sally McKinnon, Wayne Clifford (the volleyball game) are Kingston neighbours and the movie showed them before I met them – genuine pre-nostalgia. And flashes of the Coach House, Victor in palmier days. It was also weird to hear bits of The Martyrology that far back and I had a sudden image of your poetry capturing you like the Minotaur in the labyrinth – and started wondering what is the relationship of someone to the mythology they make up? Anyway.

Best, Matt.

still
for Lea
still

a road
a rod

a walk along

a long day
a dying night

an art
a log

a journal that is right
here
          ere i begin[2]
among the streets & houses stand around me
How Land over the bridge
(du pont) to Daven's Port
& in between a sea (mer)
Wal
         full tragedies are played
accomedies
                         points of view: St George & St Clair
never meet
                        (he goes to College & becomes Beverly)
fits together in its own sense
St George to separate
Admiral & Huron   history
i should've traced
                                    race
against race
against
                      time
rimes of
coincidence
                         (sense arrived at in
a later reading
latter writing
related rewrite of

tone

note

placement of
St Ick or Ylus in
the hierarchy

St Iff if if fits

(alternate spellings
suggested by
George Pal in
Dr Omic's St Andard Dictionary))

SWITCH

---

i live on Brun's wick
so named 'cause it stuck out
thick as his legendary stick
into that wal of water flowed
around the foot of Casa Loma
licked its way between
the hill that castle stands on &
Russell's Hill
                                        or south
stretching round the ruins of what was
Harbored
                        Harbour D
(a harmony)
only puns someone says
i says glimpses of another truth
'nother story worth the tell
'll do as well as Mag Mell
Olympus or
Shanghalla
all the old bars the saints'd gather at
this new one comes into our ken

                                understand (?)

i 'understand' all i didn't see before
connect these fact zones
create fictions
as someone (Brun?) did before me
if i read the map aright
'Brun's wick ken'd al[l]'[3]

set ablaze by light
it was the light!
a candle
            (Kendal)
burning

hierarchies suggested in a reading

Wal Mer's pa Dina Madi'[s] son
(her one &
only)   images of
ancient lineages

St Orm the saint of ships & seas
was he Wal Mer's father
Dina Madi's son
& if the one
then all these names could be
nicknames
for claimd similur things

(Wal Mer stretches south
into the bluer strait
streets
            houses lived in in my time
short tho it's been
one-third gone
still learning
trying to move on)

more than the grand gestures aspired to
actions give the truth to speech
content of a daily life
                                    our struggle
(ideals arrayed against the actual i deals) each morning
step out that door
onto this wick forms part of the shore
head north for the bridge
rise early
get to work before the sky turns grey with smoke
worlds of dreams & felt feelings
memories evoked of childhood despair
lost loves & lustres in this present world they are too present in
struggle to return them to the past again
archaeo logically

walked today   west thru snow   across Dupont
frozen streets/seas   thot then of Kit James
dead this past year
caught myself (briefly) wondering
'what's Kit doing?'
but he is done
one takes so long accepting
the death of friends/
                              /relationships
new twists your life takes
'in the inner circle of communication
the poet is opposed on two sides of thought'
& i am mourning his passing
                                                  caught up in the snow
Spadina
          a dirt road
trucks rumbling north for the subway's construction
underground
                    underworld
under wal
          mermur
murmer
          mer made memories
white world of whispered presences
(Kit?)

death's   deed's   done
dēath's   dead's   dōne
d'ath's   d'ad's   d'n

& gone

          'gin ag'in th'n

on

   as snow's gone
spring's come
changes tone's tune
my foots moved   on
the poem accumulates its clarity
its imprecisions

decision:
lift my foot
in march
out the snow
fresh fallen
set it down in april
when the flow
resumes

it is
enough

i would be
done
with all this
dying

would wake my friends
from
their dreadful sleeps of
false
reason

reason enough to mourn

reason enough to rail against a world

no use getting hung up on a word

no use not speaking

say it

& then

(moving this very spring
north to Warren Road
above Russell's Hill & Poplar Plains
above the port that Daven named
the ford where St George laid his bed
hoping to woo St Clair there
she lies north of me instead
impervious to his need

between Poplar Plains & Russell's Hill
some evidence of war &
whatever battle fought there
ends where these two come together
north of the port the bridge now crosses[4]
as this bridge must
connect two states of consciousness
written weeks apart
form a link your mind can follow
paths my thots had taken
transparent connections
'and' composed of forty-two words
makes it possible to travel from
'the bridge now crosses' to
'walk thru the park past the castle on my way to work'
deleting quotes (take up this speech again)

southern fringe of Forest Hill
ravines & bridges
                              (under & over)
another bridge
                          pont
pointed along it as i walk
angered by this morning's meeting
not really part of this poem
part of my life only
only part of the life this poem grows from
my own)

early july day
heading north from Toronto
Ebenezer   Wildfield
crops already taken off the land & bundled
sheep grazed gullies
summer sequences
first herds long gone from these barns
outside the city
                          numbers replace the names
subdivisions of a larger purpose
a reading changes
left at Chinguacousy Township 31st sideroad
right at Sandhill
                          north east on the 6th line
                                                Peel Regional Road 7
                                                Airport Road

3 names for just this one path chosen
sped thru Mono Road
past the left turn to Inglewood
down the hill & into Caledon East
paused to take note of the poem

when you travel on the naming changes
Caledon left   Albion right
i drive the border line
signs warn of deer
over the hills
                    Mono Mills
pause again the road's renamed
Dufferin County 18
                              take note
as i have before
                        invoked its signs if only partially
i seek to inscribe the net of names & numbers encloses me

401 west to Kitchener
pass thru escarpment south of Halton Hills
cliffs to the left
edges of
perception   re
new ways of
sea
    ing's
                      old line's
ghost geography
sail the lost lake bottom
Ellie & me   a thousand other cars
cross the crossed out
ross the rossed out
sea cedilla
softened slipping under
disappears in eternity

we will not drown in this july air
tho one hurls one's lines
as a drowning man
or a falling fool
might
                  praying for
connection
some bridge between himself & the void that threatens

drivin' long
writin' poems that come out song
sound tracking a life

Galt Preston Hespeler
they are all gone
one sign now
so many forms set my teeth to clicking
semblances of speech
                                        change
even as you pass them

driving Huron County
pass thru Shakespeare   Stratford &
the river Avon
language & its shapers
colonization of the Huron tongue
i find i cannot stop these readings

'he reads too much into it'
'he read the signs aright'
'i stayed up half the night'
                                                'doing what?'
'reading ...'

when Victor's mother died
he sent out the card that read AWAKE

these words are simply signs
signs i read as other words
messages i saw that time
wrote the phrase
'clues to unlock the secret mind'
thinking i hid the key
the tumbler's clicking awakened me

up before dawn's missed
tracing cardinal signs
North Easthope left
South Easthope right
we are driving into that east our hope resides in
what maps yield

dictating lines as they occur
revising when the moment comes
on   headlights
blurred by fog   ellie's hand
shapes the letters so unlike my own
infinite variety of form & pressure
indexed by the measure chosen

Nith River
New Hamburg to the left
Wilmot Township
sky lightening in the east
the most & least that could be written of
put an order to the mind's perceptions
make them mine
d to e
            shift
work with those occurences extend
dependent on that play to say the line ends or
continues

second take   september 3 76
Forest Road passed beyond
the boundary of a city
sequences fall   Stratford
Shakespeare
                    New Hamburg next
'Little Europe'
                      South Ontario
the counties go   Perth/Waterloo/Huron/& on
it's Toronto i return to
'r onto toro 'n to T.O.
ronto Lord
let my praise or love of thee
substain me when death comes
tho there be no greater plan beyond our lifespan
no plan even then
let that be enough

(ending on a definite note
moves the poem forward
like a foot
              a foot note

movement out of Huron County into Toronto
into your presence Lord
am i Tonto or Jingles to your kemosaby
your Wild Billing
i am charged with so much
so much i owe to you
any chain of words could lead me speak to you
as if i were Palongwahoya
charged with his mission once more
to make the whole world vibrate in praise of you

(billing & cooing
bulling but coyly
as my father must've made his move
Father/
        /Mother must have made her move too
a priori
movement into lewd
onto logically thinking thru

                i m

                u r

                n g i c so clearly
looking out across the surface of the words today
the letters are not my n m e
no thing is my n m e
tho evil lives in various guises
it's i s i's n m e
narcissus as it was so long a go
                                        e go
              and maybe even i go
                                        o go s poe goed
                                        edgarrishly
                                        all'a narcissistically
so u go
but u wonder y go
as hugo ball did
when e died e rose to heaven
& his friends said 'did. he is done.
d one & only hugo ball's bell billowed boldly BULLONG
BELONG
BE LONG TO SING MY SONG
TO YOU LORD'

flying out of
'TIME OUT'
the referee cries
'VOWELS'
so disconsonantly

u 'n a me

u name me
'i forget you'
i name me anew
claim my signs
my me
m a r t
in the word mart
the word m art
yr ology
the ology
word ology
like some old bop phrase haunts my dreams
ornithology
horn it
Ornette Coleman C.O.

le man is bird or parker
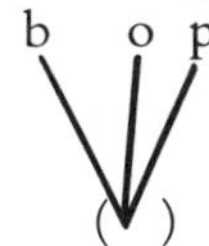

bp's me
but what is it exactly comes together)

so lord a
solo rd. as ol' ord

'je suis m. ord ...'

'merdre!'
(the choice of course
w or d
(doubled u
& l's 1
(singularities present in a word)
doubled you aligning one with one)
lord

d's common

(l l or u
u) or d
equates

eek waits
which is the fear of
devilment
deceit
'a bee see de evil in the false flower'
alpha/beta calls me to salvation
culls me out
de vine from which i flower
from which i speak my wonder into the world

'that's awe full'
taken as a compli
meant for me)

'for mi dable!'
other persona
nother name
another frame of reference

'how high the moon'
tuned to a different ear
differen' tearing of the page
an ordinary stage in the
e quations

(ord
i
nary st age in thee

'who's he?!'

(i don't mention all of them)))

AN NEX'
LADIES & GENTLEMEN
SOME HISTORY OF THE ANNEX
TORONTO
1880 & earlier

(to illumine
                         the factual
overlays the actual world i see)

Spadina
              'a sudden rise of land'
built by Dr. William Warren Baldwin 1813
160 feet wide
connecting his home on Spadina Hill to Lot Street
later renamed Queen
running up the right hand side of Lot 24
acquired thru his marriage
as Lot 25 was acquired when Elizabeth Russell died
willed it to him
controlled then all the land from what is now Dalton
east to present day Bedford
north from Concession 1 (Bloor) to the C P tracks
200 acres of prime desirability
influenced as he was 'by
the feudal feeling
which was second nature
with most persons in the British Islands
some years ago'
wanting his position to be such that people would say of him
as Dr. Scadding did
'there will always be a Baldwin on Spadina'
immortality
forgotten by his sons' sons
broke the land up in real estate deals
Walmer Road Estates (subdivided in the 1880's)
the curve from Bloor to Kendal being nothing more than a come on
a country lane feeling to lure the suckers in

november 2 76
drove down to Harbourfront to hear Wayne Clifford read
remembering eight years ago
the room on Brunswick Wayne & Juli lived in
i'd visit them
talked often
walked the tree lined streets enclosed our poems

Sean on Howland
                         Dave UU on Huron
Joe in the old coach house on Walmer Road

later
i moved back & forth
Hazelton in Yorkville
Howland on the edge of Seaton
Brunswick & Admiral
Walmer to St George & back again
reverse ordering of streets
pen creates its names activity a line
thru history
above these family tree lines

november 3 12:56 a.m.
image of Juli in that room beneath the eaves
sadness in the form the lips take
longing that pervaded
filled up the syllables a count
images touched on
snow   Sibelius Park: 1966
flickers
conversations played thru
i know more people than i can attend to
live in two communities
the one i make my daily life in &
these friends   writers   struggle as i do
make a mend
join the torn letters of the language
leaf fall
which is the turned page the prose says

atop the hill on Bathurst
look back over Howland Plains
jumbled view
two-story houses & broken fences
the full weight of civic sprawl assaults you

funny the way the language lies

more than two stories to all these houses
impossible narratives i could never tell
most of us are second story men & women
echoing lives lived second hand
lost at the second rate

there was a toll gate stood
corner of Davenport & Bathurst

the toll-taker's house still exists
hemmed in by all that was non-existent then
when the carriage trade plied these roads

scale changes
in a hundred years
my grandmother
born 1885
has seen man fly
faster & higher than she could ever dream

a platitude perhaps
reassertion of what's obvious
we dull our senses
overcome by the immensity of it all
switch channels on the second flight to the moon
barely notice the photographs of martian sunsets
consume such awe in full diffidence

Brun left here because of it
went away
fell asleep in Thunder Bay & dreams
body mined for silver he contained
drained by the very people should have praised him
raised him to sainthood
St Brun
              echoed slightly in St Utter's son
St Ubborn
                    puns
spun out the fabric of the word
i mine the language for the heard world
seen scenes unfurled by such activity

january 10th 77
drifts across Davenport & Bathurst
cars abandoned on the street
reported to me over the phone
stuck in the hills of Dufferin County
outside a storm rages

there is a world grows on this page
as r ages a st emerges
passed thru to the u age
significances of l'an g
restated

thru the vowel route we trace the change
Brun was Bran in the older days
raven who claimed a domain
north of the arctic circle
south where the bones of Utnapishtim lay
in Dilmun   if he ever died
Bran who was also Cronus
Saturn by another name
who 'sleeps within a deep cave
resting on rocks which look like gold'
'sleep is the bond forged for Cronus'
whose dreams are full of prophetic power
in his home across the Cronian Sea
wind blown waters of the North Atlantic
parallel with the north Caspian
47th parallel (approximately)
mentioned by Plutarch 75 a.d.
evidence of an older tradition
placing Brun near the mouth of the St Lawrence
'this sleep being devised for him by Zeus
in place of chains'
he awoke
strode inland
lived out some few million days
fell asleep again
in the waters off Thunder Bay
as he had awakened once before
recorded in that history of St Brendan
echoes the Bran or Brun i've come to know
came to an isle in the midst of the sea
a giant sleeping there awoke
hooked a cable on their boat & towed it
till the cable broke &
they sailed on
came upon a land so vast
they could not cross it in forty days &
turned back
never reaching the ocean i was born by

this land the titan slept in
one of the gods before the gods we know
beyond the watery barrier of the North Atlantic
'in a mysterious castle surrounded by a waste land'
watched over by Bron the castrate Fisher King

'wounded & immobile,
neither living nor dead'
an Otherworld reached by water
where the dead glide in their gray ships
'CANADA
THE SLEEPING GIANT TO THE NORTH'
as i read in one magazine when just a kid
Saturn Atlas Albion Cronus
Lord Mother
Lord Father
Bron
        Bran
                Brun
                        Brendan
                                bring me
even now as we say
as we did millenium ago
'God is dead'
i would awake thee
would ask the proper question if shown the Grail
'whom does the Grail serve'
i am your vessel too
i serve thee

Brulé was the first recorded whiteman to see Ontario
1615
        first cartographical sketch
the Molineux map of 1600
spoken of as the Lacke of Tadenac
'the bounds whereof are unknown'
Champlain's map of 1613
names it Lac St Louis
or Brodhead's history
where Lake Ontario appears in 1615 as
Lac des Entouhonorons
or variously
Kanadario
Lac des Iroquois
Lake Catarackoui
Lake Cadaraki or
Lac de Frontenac
signifier tacking back & forth
because of the shifts in the signified
the white explorers' knowledge of reality

'the great earthquake of 1663
wrought havoc in many parts of Canada
and in the east
whole rivers disappeared and
others altered their courses'

an early map by Pouchot
shows a 'crenated barrier of high mountains'
beyond Toronto
that 'crumple down into hills on the lake shore'
west of La Riviere Aucredie
(the Credit as we now know it)
mountains that never seem to have existed
tho the watershed is there
possible traces of an earlier tradition
cloud range touching earth
birthed a story of such mountains
of the beings lived there
Pouchot drew what he heard

i write as i hear
often there is nothing there
beyond a rumour or a legend
sounded
                the ground is
noise
           silence as it interrupts it
bissett in '64
visited me on Brunswick
described a technique he used
sitting in a room
wrote down conversations that occurred
focussing the ear at random
a writing of a listening

history
                   the white man's record
indians had their own legends
saw the whiteman as interloper
rowed in with death
into their world
as the french viewed the englishers
intruders in the land they'd come to claim
white v.s. white
took sides

French & Huron
English & Iroquois
H & I
twisting round of speech
mirrored them
each in each
we talk of history honouring our claims
what we claimed without honour
set out to 'tame' the New World
what was Old World
with its own legends
we name as fits our purpose
shape language to our own ends
all the lies, dishonour, death & treason such a use portends

E & F }
H & I } natural enemies in the 1620's

& God of (the many) (no) names
who is (the one) (the many)
(above) (around) (inside) all
(watched) (did not watch) over everything

God of names
who is all over everything
i read it different ways

Father (G)
Son (H)
Holy Ghost (I)
is part of we
a trinity
one step beyond the nuclear symbiology
ringing in the race trace of memory

G(od's) host (his many) or
G H (I's oly ost
(O *s(ain)t* I's capitalized
Gilgameshing the immortality trick
i lowers my case & sights
(the train of thot
lurches to a stop
(St Op is standing in the station))))

Niagara raga in
the night

silver moon
                    a sliver
l(u)siver
              falls & phalls
scar of cars moving
head slight glare
tail slight pulling away
pen t' up
down stroke the hand
o.k. eh
            la plume de ma taunting
under the skin's kin to
will & can do canto
as much then as seems necessary

months later
studying a map described the voyage Brendan made
saw the legend printed where Canada came to be
'Land Promised To The Saints'
rumours i had followed thru the half light of vision
from Brun to Bran to Bron to Brendan
Bran ab Llyr
protector of bards
king of the infernal regions
whose magic cauldron brings the dead to life
Bron who sailed westward to the Land of Beyond and
St Brendan
sailed thru the Outer Hebrides north to the Faeroes
west to Iceland & Greenland
passed the crystal column thru the thick white cloud
south to Newfoundland &
Brun   who sleeps now in Thunder Bay
husband of Dina Madi fathered him St Orm
saint of ships & storms
as Bron was the sailor of mysterious regions
focus out the haze of legend dreamed reality
saints come to be
                          a destiny
driven   despite myself
into the Don Valley

Don who was the mother of the Celtic Pantheon
called Dana by the irish
(from whose lineage Dina)
companion of Beli the Great
(Bran his nephew)
Children of Don linking with the Llyr family
Dina marrying Brun
i found a map lead me
thru Toronto's streets
into another reality
studying the night sky in wonder
recalling how (October 1970) i watched
'the shinie Casseiopea's chair'
Casseiopea the welsh called Llys Don
'Court of Don'
'known as the Celestial W when below the pole
        and the Celestial M when above it'

  M
polaris
  W

turning round the centre of the sky
i turned the 'Laconian Key' &
'E'en as a folding door, fitted within/With key,
is thrown back when the bolts are drawn'
i saw
        then
ten years & more after the poem begins
the simplest letters lead me
i am brought back
thru language
                        home
closer to the older $\frac{\text{Me}}{\text{W}^{\text{e}}}$
wind
        shaking the house
6 a.m.
sky light in the south-east
(why does it sound like a beast is howling?)
here on the hill above the harbour
i woke frightened
woke as the leafless tree outside my window shook
read as omen the stark black branches
the leafless book

noise of Brun waking
breathing over the city sleeps
6:10 a.m.
Tiwaz crosses 'over on a spruce limb'
onto the .Earth.
'as a boat over the ocean'
'over the wind falls'
flat out over the Toronto hillside
across the lake 'in the enormous distance of his cruise'
Tihwaz & Brun
lightning flash in the full window
filled lost
gone then & forgotten
gods
  except by those of us who barely know you
rumours reach us
states of mind
      we write down the cosmic gossip
line for line in the dawn of another day
frightened by the sheer noise of your making
of how you bring your name back again
in the light
in the lightning sky
dawn Dana
     it is not Tihwaz day
Brun's outline disappears against the hillside
only the phallus shows
the phall
    from Casa Loma south towards the harbourd
-ina deedju dina
deedju
    da
     de
      di
       do
        du du

dina

dina

    (in the aftermath the wind calms

i am getting into my car & driving south

6:45 a.m.

down the hill to Daven's Port
Wal Mer's edge at dawn

sleet blurring
v is i on the don patrol
bird soul seen at a distance
wing on the holy breath blows
above & below this fifth plane
this world
wold
place of gods & men
saints fell into grace & found a home on
among the g race
human
            life's played on
a g string
teased by
                immortality
we are our selves
finally
           the saints came to see
to terms with their own mortality
never assured by ultimate conclusions
or reassured
                    by knowledge of the end
casting our shadow thru illusions of time &
history
simply to be part of creation
making in a universe of making
anew & anew
again & again
women & men
until the beginning
until the end
until
            '& then')

west train night
more réal to row 'n to sail
to more owe a l l
is one
                  litter all e

& e
                            'e
move
                    (the o v over)
me   (seen in the window)

in the wind the words swing
back & forth
the signs
                                        hazardous connections to their signifieds
'st orm's brewing up a'
cup of coffee
i should never have drank.
drunk!
                      'drink?'
think & then the n
introduction to the other half

in the window?

b n inside this car
(n y reflected back?)
a & z
outside the head's reflections
(looking in
side) by side

i'm i

i me'm i

je suis
s e
            (false
(hopefully))

propositions in prepositions
whole sentences on the surface of the page
SHOUTING (occasionally) JUST TO BE HEARD

read but blue

the wind
blew but black

clouds gathered the
signs swung erratically
words quivered
on the tongue
a growing feeling of unease in
the stomach

window covered
half naked on the bed
n to y exposed from
the waist down
i's i
& i's unable to
keep the i's eyes open

all four are closed &
cannot see each other

in the mind the words swing
back & forth
the signs
hazardous connections to their signifieds
are severed
re-connected by the dream's logic

an erection becomes as big or little as it needs to be
encompassing the thot within it

tomorrow casts a hook into the brain
reels us forward into today's real

yesterday was more réal
to day to ron
to day do
ron ron

runs ahead of us
stands in one spot while we run to catch it

this is the notion of choice

this is a voice speaking
reflecting in reflection

metaphorically the page is a window

it's not

i try writing on the glass &
the ink won't hold
ideas
the mind won't hold
writing i try in the dream &

this is a pen moving on paper

metaphorically this is a pen moving on paper

gesture

memory trace

place to place &
a poem because of it
part of a poem this time
not always the case

shaped mounds of earth beside the track
in a park beside the track as we go past
under the melting snow in the park
shaped mounds of earth emerging from under the melting snow

it all goes

drifts & shifts

in the wind & mind

signs

dark clouds in the evening sky

blowing up again

storm

all day saturday
sean, thomas a., steve & i
tramped the hills of Caledon

down to the mill at Cataract
out across the bridge along the railway tracks
ice caves above the water's plunge
sean climbing the hill for birch bark for tom
'don't take too much you'll kill it'
birch, beech & book
'to write a poem on'
page
            dedication to the work at hand

above the ravine
                        looking down towards the forks of the Credit
four of us in the afternoon wind
'now this looks like Canada'
against the end of speech
discord & discard of
signs
        meeting in time
daily rhythms of a life &
voyages into the world
a breath holds
above these valleys
words
in the water's spray

'in the midst of clouds
i come to a crossing knowing'

May 12th 78

Warren Road to Ravenscroft

the road drops down

the Atlantic Ocean's a conceit
overcome in airs

enjambment of a tense & senses
move from doorways into doorways
step out into the streets of London
up from the underground
St Clair station to Golders Green
north to the room ellie & i share

reversing a thrust of history
the celtic was carried there (Canada) by Brendan
500 a.d. or (probably) earlier
stone circles on the prairie near Medicine Hat
cairns found inland in Labrador
the mind circles some truth i've circled before

the saints cross language
as the s & t
came from the middle east into England
over the sea in memory
spoken with a different stress & tone
st ress in stone
st one & lonely
different in America or Canada
in England every county forms a country
stress their r
we stress the newness of our be

hiking 'cross the northwest end of Bodmin Moor
parked the car at the disused mine near Tredinneck
pausing at the Nine Maidens
turned to stone for dancing on a sunday
later christian tales of retribution
dogs howl from the valley below
climbing the peak of Hannibal's Carn
gazing over the North Atlantic
west towards Canada
towards the origin of my be
among the circles & the stones that spawned me
millenia ago
sitting in the midst of my antiquity
in the underworld   atop
                                    the under
                          ground
    turn east again
forward into my present past
eyes ryme the landscape
scrape like a bronze age
                                              in the heel stone
half-rymed on the stone's other side
                                                          slash thru time
thru the midst of my own daze
i'll make my way
into whatever future the poem holds for me

this issue of time
                                        of ryme
- climbed Glastonbury Tor in the pouring rain
walked the ruins of the abbey there
noone spoke to me

at Chysauster
among the stone-walled huts
the fluttering souls clung 'round me
spoke in my ear as i walked the hedgerow
did not touch or interfere
merely spoke in their wordless voices
& i listened
                        answered as best i could
crouched under their roofless roofs
talking

it is like this saints
the old days speak to me
old ways have their sway
your voices absent in this english air
you seem north american who did not come from there
immigrants like all of us
take on the accent of a place
affects your own

it is Bran brands me
my own restlessness
quest in the crowded streets of London
empty stretches of the moors
search for a time your son had not visited us Lord
back to the pagan & the primitive ones
before the birth of your child changed you

do you know you changed?

the miracles dried up
direct speaking faded way
you let your son take over the day to day business of the world

in these deserted villages
among the ruined rooms
i talk to those to whom you spoke directly
the early ones who still hover here
their flickering wings around me

engine over-heating in a narrow lane near Boscawen-un
couldn't find the other Nine Maidens
left the car parked blocking the lane
tried again
                    made it
perfect ellipse of twenty stones
sun-dial finger in the centre
counts another time than mine
part of that order of which you were the master Lord
sit in the centre writing to you
sun casts the stone's shadow
between the first & second stone
1:30 by the megalithic clock
1:30 by Maureen's watch
in the ancient & the present times rymes

Nine Maidens   Bodmin Moor

Nine Maidens   Boscawen-un

Merry Maidens (Dawn's Men)   St Buryan

19 stones circling under clear blue skies
west of Land's End
beyond the reach of the ocean
within the reach of the wind
the landscape rymes again & again
(three stone circles on the eastern edge of Bodmin)

dawn the next day
sun glint red on grey blue water
sit by the harbour wall at Falmouth
boats leaving for the fish banks &
one lone man in the morning mist
in a boat in the harbour
circling
disappears towards the sea
follow with my eye & pen
i can no longer see him
sound of his boat insistent as he moves away
the hills around the harbour pick it up
bounce it back
my way

walking the huge circle at Avebury
the length of West Kennet Avenue
spoke to you Lord
gaped in the twilight at Rollright
back over the King's Stone towards the circle
circled by hills again
crossed the highway looking for the Whispering Knights
saw them in the distance among the still green plants
                                                                                the still grey men
listened to you whisper
                                                            among the stones
between the birds
                                              dull roar of traffic
in the not quite silent moments that come
your voice hums
as it must have always
Maker who spawned makers
raised these temples for you   gestures of their awe
i name the places where i found you
in a world where naming's almost gone
lost in the 'imprecision of language'
its precise gift
i make these glyphs for you
chronicles of a journey
more the tracing of rymes referred to
words
              names
ways we have of thinking thru this world you gave us
without ties
we i's that write & writ all literature
of which my voice is now a part or
more a counterpoint in a vast theme
from Golders Green to St Clair station
amid this dream of voices
these many tongues in which your names are sung
under the trees in St James Square
or outside St James north of St Clair

saints & airs

prayers

arch a is m

a connection seen
bridges tween
four to five
an afternoon & then an evening
nap

pan
pun
vowelgrrgyrations pon
pinning
down
pen
that ponders only when
the writer's home
de
script
tion

door

hall

an opening
a friend

permission

then?

change of tone

'i remember the first time when ...'
thus it is that you begin
a conversation
moves from the window to the door
over the crowded floor of
the room

too many rymes or
coincidents the placid flow of th
ink ing

in k
in g (in be
tween) h i j in the tree n
its blue
winter day
straight thru the passed glass
see it as it was the way the bird
sat there on the branch
a word in a poem
self-evident
i was seven years old

th
in
on
un
pretentious
conscious
force is
the im age

the hero has left the stage
replaced by the horror comic schemer
dreamed his downfall in his dark rage
filled with nothing but his own envy
his wish to be
there
in the longed for spotlight

paging differently

calling up the ones i still believe in
can still talk it whole[5]

emotion ideation a unity

there is a hole there
behind the w
the emptiness shows thru
these configurations spellings
evoke the feelings we cannot pretend are strangers

'the precision of openness'
a phrasing
phasing passed thru

nothing's final in itself
only tools you use
breaking thru
                         'the unyielding word'
into that world of feeling governs you

picture a man (31) narrating this poem

picture a man (36) typing this final draft

picture the man they speak of
who is almost them

picture the man who writes
(myself)
                a pose or the real thing?

& picture me
spoken of by the man telling
telling in my turn

they are all me
one way
                not me
another
               tightened focus rather
centre of a principle uncertainty

begin again then

                                    the road

begin again

                              the log's an art

begin again }
begin again } ←
begin again }

                              that song

it is a cycle i have chanted

a season in its turn

a statement of position

given its due
there's no need to hold it up to you

he is not a hero in his various guises
he is not a saint or figure to be saved
he is himself

sometimes the things we say are one & the same

he bears my name

he cannot bear it
& he shifts
h to i &
e to f
              if
stiff saint of gratitude & heartlessness
hazard of chance
never to abolish
born from death's tumble
die & be cast
                        translated
equated from you Lord

$\frac{\text{G to h to i}}{\text{D to e to f}}$
                             line being O unbending
the eternal mystery of Your presence in the world
we come out of G(O)D into the shift of probability
possibility born

b
or n (first or last
name
                    choice is false
i claim them both)
signs   monsieur ord
sighin's ici's peech
(qu'est-ce-que c'est?)
sayings worked in as a saw
seen surface surfeit

arm of God
clear light the sun
rises as in a symphony
oboes play
systematically, brilliantly, the sound
totters on the edge of language
ici le soleil
ceçi says he
seizes the line

time, t' me, tatters
shatters the shhhhh leaping
baababits of
shpeech

(name's fame's fin
ally
(alley oops)
l e
thend
&
n

am i my own last word?
conjunction tween a past world & the next?
or anti-past
a-historical
i tied to my own life of
fictions
friction rubs the daily thread of?[7] or
o
dropped from the mouth of

God
Lord
Holy
Ghost
Host?

G L H G H

7 12 8

7 8

saint

          saint

27 15 42

9

6 6

21

      3

a trinity
sliding out of
a numerology

david speaking: 'a number by itself means nothing'
i said: 'nothing by itself means nothing'
lionel was tracking the word shift: 'laughter in slaughter'
some speak of joy in all that suffering

the message was thy love wasn't it?

i do forget about that listening Lord

even in my ignorance i know
you are
          i am
               me
           em.
               ma
peel de light de lips spil.   sam tips.
i saw he keeps
ten or one t' tell to
of one lost sole no foot'l let ten or one t' speek.

eh?

          was i spit ma's lips spil()ed?

sam didn't catchem then –
but what's with all this dick tracing
pat pattin' of the past?
between the b & m's the dirth
& b & m's a birth dance of its own
part of the mirthology

reworking one book
or rebooking work one
or one work re book &
gee
    in the s peek
eek is
part of the equation
quation's hung from an e informs the scream
cream only if the c reams
eak my love & eek my fear
follow these vowel changes for what they teach me[7]

frag/
/ments re
/turn

/complete
the sense

read the lines straight down
'ken'd al[l
cross sea'

the glyph
(outline of a y or
sceptre that some sea god might be holding)
symbol of what power
rises out of bluer strait
inseparable from the sea that holds its shape

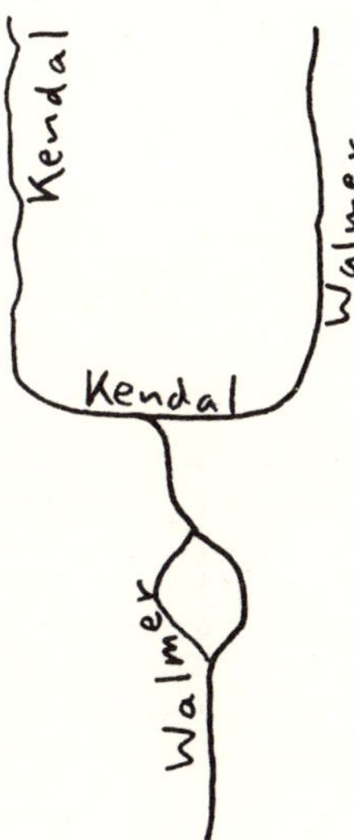

(geomancy of the streets

one-way patterns that insist automobility

foot's ascendant now
reading's
slowed
(desired's mobility of text
flex in the flux of what's actual)
translations of literal ambiguities)

below the curve of Kendal Walmer wavers
forms the sea a reading can reveal
an act u all are privy to

('a' 11 times   raised to that power
aaaaaaaaaaa
interpreted different ways
1) a sigh (as in lovemaking)
2) a sigh (as of relief)
3) a scream (as in the murder scene
– long &
lingering)

takes us where?

this multiplication
attention to a visual duration
comic stripping of the bared phrase
the pain inside the language speaks
ekes out meaning phase by phase
make my way thru the maze of streets & messages
reading as i go
creating narratives by attention to a flow of signs)

each street branches in the mind
puns break
                    words fall apart
a shell
sure as hell's
ash ell
when i let the letters shift sur face
is just a place on which im ages drift

life's a sign
beneath which signifieds slide
away from Wal Mer
Doll Town's just a step along
wade Bluer Strait
southern climes & reaches
rimes that don't make 'sense' cohere
'false' sound versus 'pure' logic
caught voicing the contradictions
hesitations
proofs of moments things aren't clear
poetry's reverse or
re-assessment of the role
rejections of pose
                                  i don't know

'too much is said from ignorance'   'SHUT UP!'

creates a movement's air
air's movement's claire   a T
mer
            L E
'the' versus 'a'
specificities of place
                                      of mood

Brun's wick's an isthmus
so named
conjuring an image of Brun
teutonic shock of brown hair
falls
his massive cock hangs off the bridge
pisses gainst the wal to fill le mer
casually
            hand resting on Casa Loma
pissing languidly

like the man i saw in Heathrow Airport London
spring of 75
                  unzip his fly &
pee
      light his pipe with both hands
at the same time &
gaze around the washroom casually
giving a separate intelligence to the thing
'a mind of its own'
                           like the dinosaurs
carried an extra brain in their tails
as if the body were
too great a distance for thot to travel

Brun's wick ken'd all there was to know
an eye stared out the head of his prick
& that stream of yellow was the knowledge flowed
down into Bluer Strait
mind freed for other things

i read here how Brun's wick went to College
like St George
                     graduating possibly the same year
but the brain his skull contained
moved in the upper reaches
far from this plane of gross physical realities
he was the embodiment of the many ways
containing as he did levels of consciousness
yet its his dick we revere
remember in a name
caught up as we were in more primitive aims
back there in our many beginnings

St Orm was born
out of the coupling of Brun & Dina Madi
twisting in her passion
outline you can still trace
Lake Ontario north to Forest Hill
writhing in the midst of Wal Mer
we're heading back there
underground
                    into that womb St Orm came down from
down to earth

Brun: 'sky goddess
        it was good to know you'
                                        (grins)
        stretches out beside her
underneath the bridge i cross
to work
          analyzing dreams
un rêve du pont
                    'i'll sleep on't'

living this last week with James T
lies down three times a day to dream
waits for the vision to come
unbidden from the unfettered mind
seeks to lose control of what he can
so what controls can rise
out of that regioned memory we know third hand
reflected back in waking
structures of the everyday
constraints & chains we do not question
till they choke us
                    bind us in
& we are screaming for our freedom
as only unfree men & women can

to treat with respect what sleep brings
the pure moment's seeing
& the seer's role
                    to read aright the brain's light
freed from constraints of consciousness
residues arise
                    what cannot be absorbed
we needs must deal with in our daily lives

sitting down today
map of Toronto spread before me
Warren Road ends at Kilbarry
did i read there a warning of my death
a sign
          realized i could read it either way
walk out the front door
turn then left or right
north to where Kilbarry takes my life
south to clear Clarendon 'n down
town tow
to Lake Ontario
or go straight ahead
thru Lyn Wood
over Poplar Plains to the Avenue
& up then to talk to   St Clair

living as i do there is that choice of confidants

St George lives under the bridge
like some billy goat gruff or common troll
waist deep in the Bluer Strait
he waits for you
feigning sleep

(when tiredness sets in
the urge to write disappears
i dsappears
ds appears
dsultory
dspairing
(dis for des?
dese for dose?
'i'll trade you two verbs for a noun'
dstnct but unntellgble))

fragments

                    bursts of song or thot

'more like static on a radio'

my life
& then these fits of sound

eruptions

interruptions

i'm tired
LOrd yr
HIrd hand's tired of this
rd.
ave.
blvd. or
lane
path
st. i walk this way with words
the St. i follow or am followed by

t he
hee hee
ha ha
ho ho
tho i know its no laughing matter some days
a sum of ways
weights the measured writing of the poem

ave

ave

ave to you St Orm

even as the days turn colder
i write s i c
older in my turn
all then
ew
(St Hat's fit top'r in t)
we
& then again
ewe
you
u
(i sang that song to my sister in the 1950s

(si(gh)))

                St Er or
                St Ersi
& maybe St Error
to forgive divine di bitter fruits its grown
sons & daughters who would spit on thee
for thy human frailties
thy lack of divinity
forgive them & forgive me both
i am the heir
a parent in my turn
should i choose to let that flame burn thru me
i can
         dled tho i be by awareness of my frailties
my wickedness
bless me Mother/Father bless me
if sister be St Ersi
what sainthood's left me?

none.

                yet i do not fear thee
Lord of the one duality
i simply speak
& in my speaking know thee
                                        the e
ternal turn all
humankind shall know

hum an'
sh   kind
all know

hum an'
sh   kind
all know

hum an'
sh   kind
all know

hum an'
sh   kind
all know

hum an'
sh kind
all know

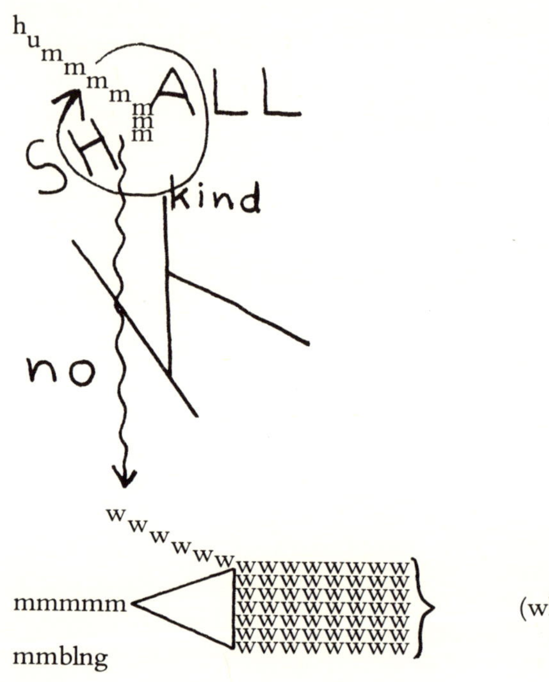

1948

'what he say?'

drowned at sea

supposedly

1955

'neki hokey'

voice music

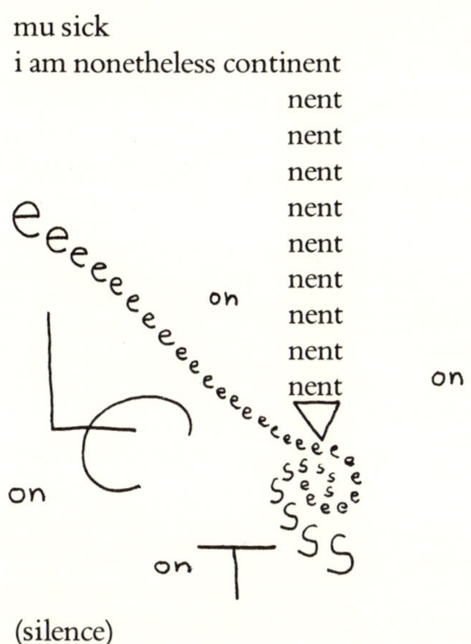

a fly crawls the base of my window
flies buzzing by my left ear

i am sitting in my room
writing out tunes my head takes
turns in the brackage of language

ua ua ua

ua

ua ua

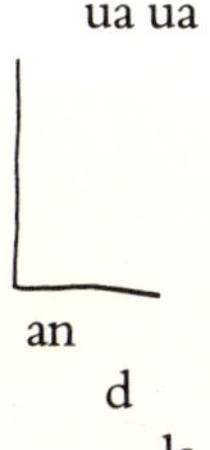

an
d
le

c (pronounced K)
i left burning in the poem
an alternative to
cursing
                    cruising endlessly among the letters
seeking the connecting streets
the St Reets that inhabit this plane
cruising at an altitude measured in megathots
an attitude
                    a particular point of view
bird's eye
                    flying in the fall sky
south

flocking

flecks to the eyes

a flexing of the mind
no need to hide in the blind to see them

flax
the crop the Nichol boys grew
middle 1800s
when they came from Ireland
Salem first
                    then north to South Ontario
my great great grandfather & his two
brothers
                    mills burned down
three times
                    moved west to Portage La Prairie
separated
                    one to stay there
two to go   south
to North Dakota
split up again
                    sons of one to remain &
my father's father & him to go
north into the flux of history

Canada

an ordinary life of strife & suffering
nothing you could salvage for the flicks
nothing extraordinary for a movie or t v show
no thing
except the living
& the will to go
                                        on
with honour
another hour day week month year Lord

sum day You'll take us away
as i was promised
never believed
believed in You Lord
did not believe
the comics i read in sunday school
only in You
only in You
only in You
only in You
only in You
only in You
only in You
only in You
only in You
only in You

that insistence

that phrase's
praise of You

only of You

only of You

only of You

from the core of us
a chorus
Horus
          God
                    Father
                              Son

one & only in Your many names
Mother
            White Lady
                        Goddess
the less is known of You
the less is sung
You grow old & lonely when Your children leave You
vindictive its said
rain Your rage upon our heads
bring an end to our worlds
our selfish living

selfish is where the self is H
attains that link between the ones
forms llord
            the mahayanna view
having reached a point of unity with heaven or with God
we must place ourselves
again
        into the world

forward is a for world stance
the human thing to do

living now in Tertiary times
fog lights on the Allen Expressway
Wilson Heights Boulevard North
i am following an expression
as far as it will take me

street names
a series of street lives
lights
        follow the leader on the tape i talk to
hit the stop switch
when the driving's more demanding than the speech

ESSO

            S O B

if i become well known
i become a brand name

fame makes its own claim on you

anonymity gives the attic view
as Emily knew so clearly

who wants to be a household word?

OLD DUTCH CLEANSER

the absurdity

mind rambles on fame or
a meditation on names
i reinvoke
                    things
a sing of
                    idiosyncracies

Dufferin Street north of 7
the land changes
hills rise in the midst of farmland
autumn stands of trees
barns tumble in slow motion
years in the disintegration

to 'make a name for one's self'
as tho what one were born with
granted
were not enough

to somehow be
carried beyond one's span

& thus we cease to speak to
our friends
                    be rooted in
community
some immunity
munificence that friendship brings
'sins' of 'private writing'
i speak to those who know me
those who don't know me
i hope they speak to me

'you shouldn't speak with your mouth full'
let that insistence that is content take you

themes return
cyclical   encyclical

5th sideroad
Mono thru Adjala
turning right & south to Hwy 9
left over the King Township Line
of poetry
                    boundary
                                        time
autumn
                describes a shift in scenery
weight of leaves falling
                                                    trees
grace
                    an empty splace
Schomberg   27
sky turns darker grey
day draws to a close
those on my back
what's closeted in me

sunglare speedsign lies behind
dark lines of hills & trees
be for me what they will always be
unobtainable horizon

crossing 400
on towards Newmarket
the day grows steadily darker
i feel farther away than ever from seeing
what it is i look for in these readings
sun setting behind or
clouds cover it in
world rolls on in its turnings
there is that thing within me burning
aching
                yearning
                                    longing
all the words i seek to find an object for
nouns they modify

sky falls in on me
St Reat again
his face framed in clouds
crowds who speak my name
as if they accused me
of what?

                        nothing

my dream   my guilt
my finger points out the fault in me

rolling out of Toronto
westbound trans-continental
11:39 under the Maple Leaf sign
awake to watch the others sleep
passing thru the CN yards north of Finch
midnight
                October 19th October 20th 76

the moment of the poem draws near & passes
rain against the train window
against the t
rain
        inside
words ride the eyear connection
tonight that seems enough for me

leaving the last lights behind
somewhere north of King City
night encloses me
the page
              'til the next ring of
words
           lights
wakes me

Sudbury in early morning
Capreol & beyond
mile after mile of trees
skinny birch & evergreens
frozen pools of water & the snow
thousand mile forest
surest wood i know

walking the platform at Hornpayne
no clear ideas in mind
it is like that sometimes
life
      the poem
parallels from which words flow
connections that are made
aid you in your journeying

turn & return
light slowly fades
night aboard the westbound train
conductor passes thru
'last call for dinner'
tracking the inner view
interviewing myself
an intra view
which craft i am apprenticed to
interface
place of this solitary voice in the world chorus

waking from a dream
berth sways so i can hardly write
stayed awake half the night
reading
            writing
                        rhythmic tack of talk
pen scratch
lay back to let sleep catch
morning

Winnipeg

H origins
remembered names

Fort Rouge

St Boniface
he of the happy face
eternal smile
saints that were there
over the river in
my childhood

the presbyterian boy who
eschewed the ritual view
but not by choice
voiced in the hard-backed pew
hymns in the blank-walled sunday mornings
over the Assiniboine & into memory
Empire Hotel we stayed in
second time we moved here
1957
        mother crying
hated the house we rented
hotel we stayed in
Dea & me
                the two kids still at home
we felt depressed too

taking the bus to Portage & Main
no one left here who knows me really
no one i could drop in on
call up on the phone
only the memory of teenage loves & losses
wandered the streets
half-expecting someone to call my name
tricks of memory
frames of reference
emotions i thot of as most me return
i am that boy again   briefly

left on Broadway
Mordue Brothers Funeral Home
mort ou
the skeleton of Fort Garry
across the street from Union Station
back aboard the train &
let it carry me
out of the past crowds in on me
Portage Junction
Pembina Hotel
away
        over the prairie

Fort White to the south-west
smoke stacks i still recognize
biked out there   age 8

H was my home then
Wildwood Park Fort Garry
behind me now
smoke drifts east from the cement factory

heading west to Saskatoon
my brother Bob was born there
my sister Donna died
six weeks old
                    as i almost died
six months old
Rupert Street in Vancouver
choking to death for no reason
the no reason was inside me

3450 Wilkes
one mile from Carman Jct
squat white bungalow
nobody i know
                    noted in passing
their lives go on
                    we touch obliquely
only in this poem

Wilkes Avenue paces the tracks
miles beyond Winnipeg
gains the designation 427 at mile 10.6
ends at the turn to Headingley
changing to an even narrower dirt track
signified by the proper noun Wilkes
modifying the general term Road
past farms & fields
unfrozen sloughs
light snow the black earth shows thru
far as the horizon
i read the road
e to o
runs on beside me
angles off finally to the left
disappears
marked only by the trees & buildings
clustered miles apart
it is the and for

e o

e o

Dacotah

farmer's fields

furroughs form a 45 degree angle with the track
change to parallel
& back   up to 90
back to 30
                    last ploughing before the first snow came

criss-crossed the west with my family
1944 to 63
dad working the CN
moved again & again
Vancouver Winnipeg PortArthur
Winnipeg Vancouver
shift in street names
Blenheim
                    Rupert
                                   H Section
Marks
             Morley
                            Oakwood
                                              Oak &
Cambie   moved then
                                         finally
out on my own
Comox in Vancouver   Hazleton in Toronto
then that circle of streets enclosed me ever since
within the boundaries of the Annex

Saskatchewan

distinct column of red light
stretched between a higher cloud &
mass of grey vapour
blocking the south-west horizon

sun setting   momentarily seen
red finger raised   St Orm's face
grey with grief & rage

flames leap up from the field we pass
offering of leaves & grass to you Lord
smoke billowing away

momentary vision

sails
        or
the outlines of nameless things

clouds & blue

Atwater

sky

barnyard lights blinking on

black fields
pale yellow grass

definitions

(e o   e o)

asleep thru Saskatoon

of what's past

60 miles south of here
my great grandpa Leigh homesteaded
1906
        moved north from Henning Minnesota
constructed a house of sod & lumber
Viscount District of Saskatchewan
near Humboldt
with 8 of his 11 children
his daughter, my grandmother,
following him north five years later with her husband
settled near Plunkett
my mother was born

Edmonton 7 a m
day of talk & sleep

carry the poem forward
journal
                the *utanikki*

October 23 1976
reading Shiki's *Verse Record of My Peonies*
the pot of them that Haritsu & Sokotsu brought him
'Thin Ice' on the name tag
on the window of this room this morning

name tags

nick names

'bp'
'nick the prick'
'pussy'
'nicky'
all of them me
all noted in my *nikki*
adrift between the signifier & the signified
sliding thru the years
myself as definition changing

three days later
climbing into a cloudy sky
ruins that i knew are far behind
heading off
                into an unknown country
i seek   only the absolute
the instant's poem
all the contradictions present to be dealt with
saints & shadowed earlier gods
voice of Brun
arm of Dina Madi reaching
atop the cloud range & beyond
regions hinted at in dreams
where the old ones dwell
immortal   inviolate
forgotten when their names are gone
you tolerate them Lord
the many guises of your signifiers
know you are the signified
this plane flies on
over a flat country of uncertain boundary

cloud town empty &
the trail to earth destroyed
some trace of names
Knarn a place then only in their memories
like the little graveyard on the 5th sideroad
Mono Township
'restored to perpetual care'
farmers & families who struggled to build their share
forgotten now
                                        great grandfathers & grandmothers
those who died too young to bear
where i went that one day to write GHOSTS
rubbings with pencils & pens
early Ontario concrete poems
til i felt afraid or
uneasy
                    as tho i had disturbed their rest
or that day i walked thru Kensington in the rain
visited the Egyptian section of the British Museum
stood over the mummified remains of kings & queens
bodies that had found some immortality
& shuddered
                                            heard
in that crowded room
complaining voices of the dead
turned my face away & left
dismissing it as melodrama or
the stuff of which bad poems are made
troubled all that day
took the underground to Golders Green
depressed &
talked to Sean of other things to lock the ghosts away
thinking always at such times of Donna
my sister
                                        my mother's first child
dead at six weeks & what done
what deed i should remember
only her shoes i found
leather cracked & dry
in an old cardboard box when i was thirteen
with a photo of ma & Bob
her next born
rushed into Saskatoon to the photographer
in case he died too

crying after Donna's death
nothing left to remember her by
echoed her in Deanna's name
the next & last girl to be born
& Don
            when he came into this world

below the plane the clouds thin
drawn out so fine one gazes thru
onto the man marked surface of the earth
language of fixed fields
twisting courses of
Assiniboine or Red rivers
37,000 feet above Manitoba
we are moving too
above the dead who brought us here
the living let us into this world
line thru time
b.c./a.d.
                    b.d. will do
all my parents used to name the five of us
Bob Barrie Donna Don 'n De-
anna
        Donna echoed twice
her death
              sounds in our family's daily speech
our history   cycle really
acyclic   if i step outside
retain the edge of that perception

high over the Great Lakes
cloudworld hangs below us
our world awaits
below the massed & empty stretches of that place
Sleeping Giant suddenly remembered
stretched out in the waters off Thunder Bay
climbing High Street
almost every day
just so i could see his face   there
in the wolf's head that was Superior
Superior being i could never speak to
feared to disturb
                        as if he might rear up & smite me
strike me down

drifting thru the cloudworld parts to let us thru
that space between
their world & our own
some face glimpsed briefly or
my imagination wanders

Brun?

only a name recovered in a reading
riding
back again
onto the asphalt
into Toronto
Toto r onto
logically Dorothy's friend
funny animal world of barking men &
speaking dogs
recalling the shock
1973
    rereading Thornton W. Burgess's OLD MOTHER WESTWIND
echo of the voice i claimed as mine
soft slide of vowel sounds
slipping round a harsher consonantal shelf
the self recovers these echoes
vocal traces of earlier love's lives
i wrote three poems to Donna i remember
haunted by her infant face i never saw
staring at those last mementos of her
placed among the consolation letters
i made my own
unwind themselves in the brain's grey reaches
remembered or imagined pain of infant death
caught up in the sob informs my breath line
lin
  li
l & i remain
        one & one
ne gation stationed at the tongue's door
to speak of it no more

snow

        outside the plane

the voice is mine speaks again

Old Mother West Wind don't warm me now
waiting the propeller spin round
tick talk taxi to the sky
my my

a possessive case
a subjective case
the object of this proposition
presupposing readers & a faith in living
book for book
goes on beyond me
ies dies
my my my

reference stanza's end
as in a cliff you stand upon
words bunch before you
follow intuition thru
seek the new
clear fissions & a kind of fiction
achieves momentarily reality
a sigh
          my my my my

high over the cloudworld mist floats
mountain or plain concealed from view
no saints to talk to
only the flat horizon line
beyond which more of the cloudworld lies
my my my my my

                                        my
how the boy do sigh
longing a lingering theme
heme the one from whom song's spun
above the Kootenay River
below the house that Fred & Pauline bought
across the way the mountains rise
disappear in mist

was this how the saints managed it?

the day the cloudworld touched the earth
clambered down the mountain peaks
here where Columbia & the Kootenay meet
stumbled out to greet the earth-bound day

cloud hidden your face & name
tho i flew above it yesterday
sank thru the white world into this valley
part of the will to be near you
speak to you's the same
i demand nothing in return
tho its true
i wish from time to time
you'd find some way to speak to me
even that thot mocks me

your presence everywhere around us
sentences in rocks & trees
remembering London spring of 75
Paula Claire reading
her text the leaves she'd found
prints of stones
voicing lines & signs she read as sounds
notation
Mother Nature
God the Father
world's a word
you are one & the same

so many echoes in this place
Li Po & Wang Wei
a sense only
eight years since Fred & i last met
across the 2000 miles separates our day to day reality
distances the ancients wrote out of
formulating concepts of citizenry
winter snow on the black highway
when will we meet again

circling over Castlegar the next day
headed off up valley between the Selkirk's peaks
prisoner in front of me
lighting his cigarette as best he could
the deputy sheriff across from him
admiring the scenery

breaking thru fog to fly
over the flattened plain
these peaks are no part of their ranges
intrusion rather of an earthly terrain
clouds in the valleys as far as i can see
two to three hundred miles all directions from me
seated in this 12 seater Cessna
so close my knees touch his back
is to me
            handcuffs concealed from view
one valley visible below the plane's right wing
a rift or lake
in this cloud world of which i sing

the great folds or rippling of the rock
from the Selkirks up into the Rocky range
plane rocking & bucking as the air rises
lifts us up & drops us
the sheriff & the prisoner talk like old friends

maybe it's me who's out of place
displacing air by my very presence
talking tho there's no one here to listen

'he's got his head in the clouds'
'his feet aren't on the ground'
is there someone somewhere i'm talking down to?

the Rocky's trail away to the right
flying over the densely wooded slopes
barren slashes of the lumber companies
on to where the cloudworld begins again

huddled so close to earth i become obsessed
as if these were the ranges texts spoke of
earthly peaks the saints sojourned
as many months as they were forced to wait
til their world scraped the face of this other
place i call home
citizen of earth
here in the province of my birth
take as provident
those connections years extend
as images

edge of cloud
drifting in among the whitened trees
climb higher into green
straight run across this white plain then
flying thru
disappears behind you
cloudworld lost from view

above it all the dome of blue sits
peaks & ranges vanish finally
i stare thru
down to where my life awaits
no saint to live on this unsure ground
Lord you are always reminding me
some lesson in humility
instead of asking you to talk i should listen to you

corner of Alpha & Beta
Victoria B.C.
windowless building with two doors
inaccessible because of the trees & bushes planted there
heading over to Mayfair
just noting these language mysteries

546 Alpha
faded one-story frame
torn curtain draped over rusting metal bedstead
broken easychair on the front porch
just along from Gamma Street
leads off to the left
AANDERAA INSTRUMENTS 560 B
SEAKEM OCEANOGRAPHY 560 A
when one is lost in language
is one all at C?

looking thru the family bible next day
envelope postmarked March 21 1935
addressed to grandma Workman in Plunkett
faded rose petals & leaves
letter lost now in the years between
knew when i saw it
it came from Donna's grave
42 years since she died
would she have been a mother now
or would death have claimed her in some other way

sometimes i wonder if Donna's speaking thru me
idly its true
the thot crosses my mind
is this why i felt forced to find my 'own' path
back into language thru play
as tho i were learning to speak again
an owned sway
as if she were there
at play in the cloudy fields
i only know i try to follow thru
truths an attention to language yields

& ma told me
how near the end
grandma Nichol would lie in bed
singing hymns
unaware she was doing it
face lit from within

so much i admit i don't understand
are we living out a 'and' era a
time for
conjunctive reading
a shift in
the d n a
forced to grapple in a new way with
the world

talking late into the evening with Barrie & Deanna
reminding me how ma would talk to us
told us about Donna frequently
reminding us we had another sister
her first child
that she dwelt in heaven
sickly from the day she was born
the night before her death Donna smiled
ma turned to dad saying
'she'll be okay'
died the next day when ma was breastfeeding her
        the hurt

confused images

family daze

talking with Dave two days later
mountainside in North Vancouver
children heading off thru the ravine
trying to come to terms with some sense of family
a weight thru history
blood relations & the claims friends make on your mind
your time of thot
you start with that person in front of you
dialogue
acknowledgement of being
the 'real' you get into poetry is
the 'real' of speech
the fact you try to reach
pleasure some other body from your own
all this talk of
form or
meaning
an investigation
gleanings from the act of
poetry
            a noun
describes more perfectly than any other
that heightened sensibility talk should be
an act of family
gathering together like mind & feeling
in the 'real' speak
having driven from Victoria on the ferry
fog & rain over the islands & the strait
drove into Surrey
visited grandma Workman in her 92nd year
trying to image that gulf of time
talked of grandchildren
great grandchildren
her changing sense of the world
having watched a programme on space shuttles the previous night
shook her head
nothing more that could be said

explaining to someone the other day
how the saints come to me in the writing
how i speak to you Lord
                                        then as now
moments when the channel opens
my eyes fill with tears

tho i hang back from the full feeling
wonder 'is this real?'
its real when i talk to you
speak the saints by name
call my friends forth
into the instant of the poem
make connections from form
back into content

to say as i see
tho too often it still disturbs me
write around the truth sometimes
i give my trust over to the lines
i hang from
a climber in the cloud range
i don't know the one in front of or the one behind me
sense them in the line's play
a tension or an easing of the same
i let that climb continue as it may

Donna today it seemed to me
you could've been a writer
not that this action's not my own
it is
        but this business of words
of texts that pile up in a day's writing
a year's
we shared that fear of living
you died at six weeks
i almost died at six months
in that moment glimpsing you
we shared some common experience
i turned away
back into the world
never regretted it in the years since
was i too young to realize what i was getting into?

in the speak which is not speaking
when i am seeking you Lord
in the say when i let you in
no longer distanced in the cynical
i stands aside you has its way
twinned
or the limb only of your gesture

sick of the old pleadings
claim only my belief in you & nothing more
no heaven or special preference for saying
Lord i acknowledge & love you
let it be
simply that feeling & no other moves me

April 30th 77
                                        Paul phoned
'Jerry Lampert's dead'
                                                        ashes to dust
the head struggles to accept it

Kit gone
                              Jerry gone

Pat Elliot too

voices i'll miss

make my way thru this region of the known
join them in the un
country of my birth   death
carry out this trust been granted me
those few left who see a worth in the activity
songs of praise & grief
songs of joy
flow from our pens & mouths beyond us

gazing thru the car window today
clouds pile up above the 401
thinking of the lives
                        the deaths of friends
i've come to equate life & the poem
in touch at last with the real mysteries

hill

fields

words pace me

here fords

there chevs

f or d

che v.s.?
        verses re
fidelegant egress
egreter or lesser degreen or
yellownership   a matter of
de green fields
de high hills
who owns de ford
who drives de chev
y
    ellie asked
'trying to be inspired?'
do i aspire to be inspired?
is that arrogance
to seek to be one's own inspiration?
as much a sin as causing one's expiration?
do counsel me

                                        if i climbed that hill
lay down in that field atop
let the clouds drop down & cover me
would that bring me closer to thee Lord?

the days are too ordinary
the world is
too taken with itself
the word is bought & sold cheap
daily speech is the marketplace of deceit
& i have pledged myself not to bargain with thee
work my life with my own hands as best i can
accepting the help friends grant me
granting them what help i'm able
more able than i sometimes believe
i believe this life goes on
i believe this life ends
& God i ask nothing more than what those two limitations extend

but there are nights

there are days

there are dreams that portend
signs that foretell
i am for telling all i see
because it seems you asked it of me

journal entry: august 26 77
'i drive the martyrology daily
retracing lines i have already written'

driving east on 60 thru Algonquin Park
mid-October 77
Lake of Two Rivers
clouds divide the earth & sky

first snow clumped upon the trees & phone lines
dark greens & red of needles rotting
white spreads thru the trees
over the rock outcroppings
the face of nature is the face of place
not as particular but a general term

i watch the clouds turn
barely cling together in the grey sky
Hidden Intersection where the mind meets the mind
right turn left
there is no polarity if you drive straight ahead
up then into a place called heaven

this drive
drives on the physical plane
part of a general tension or persuasion
'there's too much play in that line'
by which is meant 'slack'
an s lack
absence of a feminizing fact or two

push towards H *e(a)ven*
shown in my life/writing
}

2
do become
1

note

jotting in a larger work – x
is tense is
tially shall he
this or that
posited as 'free'
will he
do drive drown
THE SUPREMES
being only themselves til
a superstar emerges

ologies
caus martyr
mologies
the head's a spin
'he's seeing stars'
minute movies or
the thimble theatre we dub 'life'
silent screens in darkened rooms
like a 'low-life' or a low mood
fragment of a cyclothymic brooding

you can sense the rep
the tition
s sense
s en s 'e's sence
'typing error responsible for suspicion'
'botch-a-you you botch-a-me'
ba be
bi
bo
bu by
'ba ba loo'
just a variation on
initial initial me

viz: 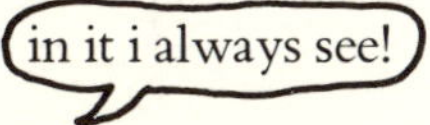

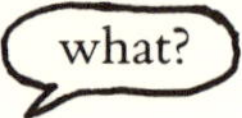

just a voice in a cloud or
a crowded room

speech of vision

initial initiate

in it i ate from
the tree of knowledge

voices that persuade invade the page
pace my own volition

evolution & me
flashing a darwinning smile
preference as the p reference
includes that mid-initial ground
bridges first & last
entrances & exits
'put in a book & titled'
'the flow of which is poetry'
my life Lord
nothing compared to yours & yet i don't compare
my life Lord
my condition

con dit: 'i on'

(ou sphere
(which is the global view
glow ball crystal vision
clear))

another con fess 'i on'

at the core us rings thru
a plurality of feeling
being two & two
relational

'why con then?'

prisoners of our frameworks really
our mental sets
backdrops for the larger drama of
our 'lives'
(parentheses because the *pair-in thesis* is
we's none of us alone)

'oh'

(tho i've moaned a poem or two in my time
its just the ignorant groan
awaking in a dark room
i didn't know the door would open
that i controlled the key
having rented it in 44 or 5
(okeanos
where the sun comes running up the hill &
i spill my feelings
swallow the bitter s pill
avoid the s wallow
acknowledge woman birthed me &)
i return
a different doorway when the passions burn brightest)

but the mind travels so many routes

over the border out of England
the landscape doesn't change

we enter another
state of mind
shift in
the ac-
cent

a messenger then or
carrier of the news
found myself
days later
in a stone circle at Castlerigg
in the centre of the peaks
listened to your voice speak in the wind
vowel noise you make
pressed against the drum you fashioned in my body

the ear takes in what the mind cannot encompass
only half believes
glib faith in your existence
under the blue sky north of Windermere
under the blowing clouds & the slowly shifting sun
where the world comes together with its history
murmur of the many of which i am one
gone soon into the many
some other one to come
questioning our place
this scheme of
things
                studying the past
the present
                future for what it teaches us
in the inhabited places of this earth
the gardens from which our speech flowers
among the images inform our poems
our history of literature
come in time to dwell in memory as familiar
so long cliché is its name
the images outlast us
the daffodils & buttercups
within the stone walls of poetry's cottages
the image bank's reopened &'s recycled
enters the world of print & passes from us
megalithic structures we call poems
left to stand on the white plane
builders' dying
growing a little older every day
in the cliché of age
sends you forth to flounder on your own
thru the world of scorn & noise
into the silent reaches of the brain
i'll let the text explain itself
leave the rest to stand
inexplicable as stone

returning to Castlerigg at dawn
cuckoos calling
grind of lorries shifting gears
up the hill towards Penrith
sun rising due east atop the one stone

thru the opening in the ring of hills
in the chill of 5:30 a.m. the light
spreads out over the valley
over the stone circle
over our still waking heads

Ellie paces the outer rim
one step two
Maureen & Steve in the living centre
'you can feel the heat here'
snow on the upper reaches of the mountains

these words these
incantations prayers & riddles
spelled out in the chill air
now as the sun reaches us
the vastness seizes us

Arthur's Table, Mayborough
Long Meg & her daughters
four of us pacing the circle there
studying whorls on ancient stone
as if a tone were struck within the brain
rings the changes
links the chains of
thot   history
mysteries that seem insoluble
the voluble presence of a silent world

driving over Hard Knott Pass
into the Roman hill fort Medeabogdum
only the sheep left grazing
here at the outer edge of what was once Rome
700 feet above Eskdale
gazing out over the valleys & the mountains
no words left at that moment i don't need them

the mind works in different gears
struggling to absorb assaults of grandeur
earth's & man's
gestures of arrogant military brutality
turned into this lonely wonder
at the top of the world

holding my breath on crumbling walls
man piled stone
amid the sheer rock weight of
mountains
attempting to be true to
the moment at hand
the thrust of the poem
the cumulative weight of your own history of a writing
pushing you into this shock of perception
it all crumbles
                                all falls away
Castlerigg at sunrise
                                  Hard Knott hill fort as sun falls
all the seasons of the earth
falling away beneath me
in the midst of this tiny poem
                                                        these few books
among the sheer weight of all literature
or nature
                            wilder by far
more enduring than these human walls & words but
in the end
simply to have said
i began them
carried them thru to
the end or
was outlived by them is   in a way to
begin to
be human

bridge shaped from fragments of older tunes
discarded   excised

november 71 (random)
voices from the record player
voices from the head
lie in the bed & make sense of it
no longer part of your vocabulary

afternoons of t's & h's
blown up from towns to the east
conscious of each song the bird sings
differences
diffidence that listening breeds

how was it there?
cloud town i mean
what was your sense of we?
social good? individual good?
was it the usual repressive society?

Halifax   Dec 4th 71
Roy & me
route 3 to Peggy's Cove
GOODWOOD   dark clouds in a blue sky
gulls   boats   instances of sequence thinking

1968
weight
as in any measure   stops
like the dropped line
disparate
the connections shatter
desperate
all that is left
said or unsaid
inside this circle
inside this moment i have lived before
what sense of time   music that i move from
i am the I i hold   turning
the imperative is the present tense
the sense of urgency moving

(saint reat
it's hard to say

you were the one i knelt before
before the others were more than a game
split my skull & showed you the dull wonders
sun travelling round me in my ignorance
had my own way of going
knowing things to do
lost sight of
til the child & i
stood by the dark line of trees
watched the tide flow backwards from the bay

4

(speaking that day of John Thompson's daughter
John's dead
                    abandoned words
fill your head
messages struggling for release
are they clearer as you grow older?))

this is a love poem for a time
moments the world lay open to the mind
you stepped thru
bodies touching as they do in sleep

i know how this seems St Reat
fictions for a time our place is

i never lied

is this what the muse is

so much skin

so many breasts & thighs

stand in the rain
[London] *May 17 1975*
Sean & i gazing up the height of
Cleopatra's needle
                    muddy waters of the thames below us
4000 years have brought it here
among a strange people
who do not worship the god it honours
another shrine stolen
another name for you known

father/mother
will i see you soon?

this poetry of place & places
traces of earlier rimes
out-takes of the muse's movement thru me
or my own grappling with a wish to speak
each one a bridge i chose not to take
reasons lost now in the years between[6]

failed lines or conceptions
voices that i bid be still
troubled by what they troubled in me
so that i sentimentalized them
gave myself a reason to reject them
threw them away
arrogant mood of self-congratulation

everything reconsidered then

take it all in
the bad & the good
the could have as well as the was
ask yourself what you're doing
where you're going in these words

(you's me
peeks out these marginalia
these footnote chains
ask myself
who took the im from mortality
accept its absence
lack of answers
try to make my feelings plain)

you do what you can
ask *of the walls you live in*
fingers & a way of loving
way of reaching not of holding on
i become revisionist in my thirty-third year
fold the old poems in
search them for clues to
earlier feelings
early incarnations

evening star over our shoulders

walk thru the snow towards our home

what is it passes thru you as the other opens
shows you the way to go
living inside each skin you meet
as if this were touching

turning round the page
walking south the view changes
the landscape remains the same
bridge d i s
carded
            vo ices
l i e
no after   no ons
blow n conscious
dif f
idence

how clou
dwha tso
c i a lwa   sHali
fax

Roy rou
tego odwo odgul
ls
      1
9 6 8
we i
g h
       tli
ke
      th
eal lsa id
insi
        de
insi
        de
wha
tiam thet he's aint

it's you before
split sun

had knowing lost t
ilstood watch

ed shaped from i n
lo n g
ero fu poftha
twastow n wasgo
odit & 3

as the disparate connections desperate
that or this
this sense am imperative

sense re a t
h ar d
we re the mytra

velling my things
sight the b
y the f r
               om excised

no vember
the t he
part t's from
each listening

it   i   your

individual the

December

me to dark boats
in dropped shatter is unsaid
circle moment of the is o f
to the others skull
round owntoof
child the tide fragments

1

record voices bed
of & t
owns

song

differences breeds

there?

mean sense good
usual 4th peg
g y's co veclo
uds any line

left
        i time I
the urgency   say
one were & me
wa y d o &
dark flow of (random) player
fro m & you h's

to the of repress
ive so c i e
ty 7 1 in instances measure

have i present moving i
lost & out of pattern
as a guide only
know this landscape
'like the back of my hand'[11]
more showed in o
f i
line backwards older
t h e
make vocabulary

the bird wea ofli ved
music hold tense

knelt than you

my going off
romtu
nes
head sense
east sings blue sequence

stops

before that before
at h e ignorance
trees

theof

sky thinking

i turn in g

g am e

d ull b a y

it move wonders

from

they can
as if they were
but

and

you long to touch

we refuse to say

, these

or
, i was

unwittingly
& did

as it must be

then

&

i'm the one
, out of

the questions like

do

& break them up again

fragments

71

voices
&
vocabulary

&

listening

was
good?
repressive

71

Peggy's

dark
of

stops

disparate

unsaid

i

present

reat

were
more
you
in
way
do

i

watched flow

spea
king jo
hn's fi
ll mes sage
sar ethi smome
ntsy ou bo
die

si fi
c tion si isso
sost and lo

ndonsea ncle
opatra s
4
   0 0 0 a
mo n gwhoano
therano therfa thermo
therthistra cesou
t-takes or each reasons failed

voices troubled so
gave
        threw arrogant everything
that dead abandoned your struggling
they is the stepped touching

know for ne
verthi smuch man
yi n ma
y & i
needle years a do shrine name

poetry of o
fmyon elostlin es
tha tby
tha tmy
                        selft
hem m oodrecon

sid er ed day
head for clearer
a world thru
as how a lie dwhat

skin

breasts

the 17 i

muddy ha vestra
ngeno sto
lenfo rofear liert
he own a now
or i what i a aw a yofthen

of words release
as love lay they
this time

the & rain

1975

gazing waters brought people
worship you
will place rimes

muse's grappling bridge in conceptions
bid they sentimentalized reason
self-co n g
ratula ti
on John
you poem open
do
    seems our
muse

thighs up of it
the known i &
movement

with the be t rouble
d t he m to t
hompso n's grow
fortoinst place
ist het he he
rego dsee
places thru
a i y e
arstil lin reject
daughter
older at h
e sleepr eatish eight
tha mesit youm ewish

cho sebet ween me
thenmi ndof below
hono ur s s oo n
tou stake

&

well

you're

marginalia

the mortality

my

you

a

not

thirty-third

poems

early

star

passes

the

inside meet

and

the

or

drove out together

(report on a state of mind)

— it leaves you
desparate. but why? you're so to say
to be
, as tho we lived our lives

you know
these things

— you know i

take the t
he ask where's you peekingt
he ask in g w
hoac ceptin glack
try i n g you
ask fingers wa
yifo ldsear chearlie
rearly even in g
walk what shows living as it bad

could yourself you remeoutfo
otno temys elf tookits
oftodoof & ofbec
o me thet hemfee lingsin
carnat i on s

start hru isy ou
inside if all &
have what goin go
fch aint he absence

answers make whatt he are aching

revision is t
old forover
the it
          the each
                    th is

in the as you're in
the immy you wall swaynot

in poems clues our snow passes
way skin were good
well doing these marginalia

ou t ow n canyo
uofofm yintos hou
lder st. owards thrutoy
outo yo uto uch

in gas words of feelings
live loving
holding thir tythir

dour yo umeett
hemor talit
ypl aininon year home
as w as t
he ot
her opens[6]

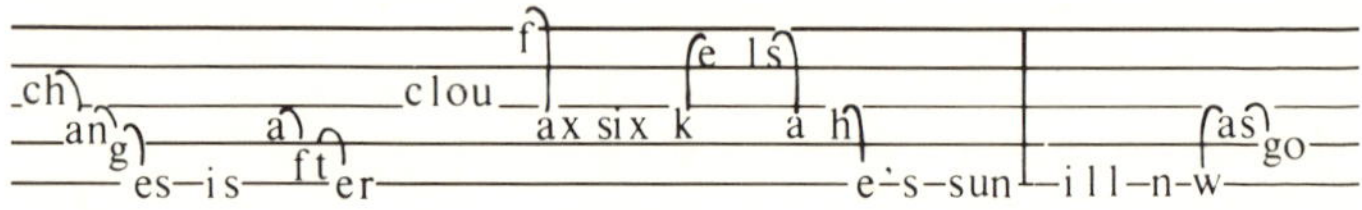

there is nothing left to be written/ /tunes head east repres-

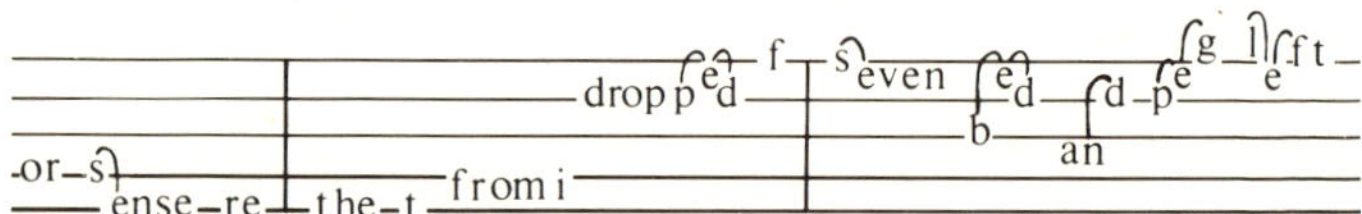

sive earlier/i still/not of thirty-third home is no g/lsa

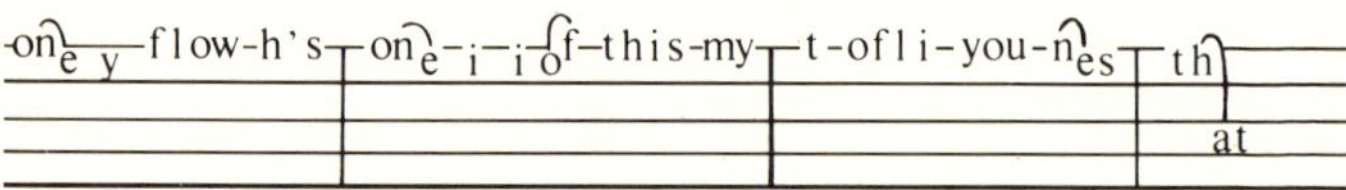

ed from twastow/the or/b excised/were(random)ive ty this

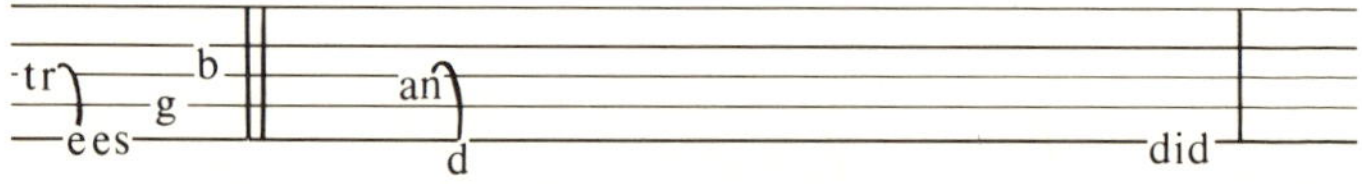

e nes//of that old life/he has said too much/ /or frag-

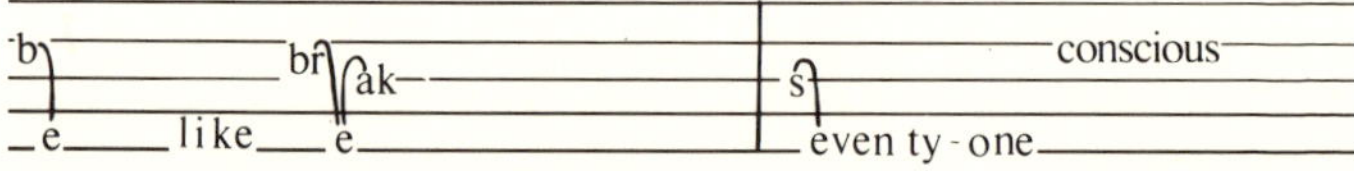

ments/tion hem a thru/own love do/lin e fingers even/ /

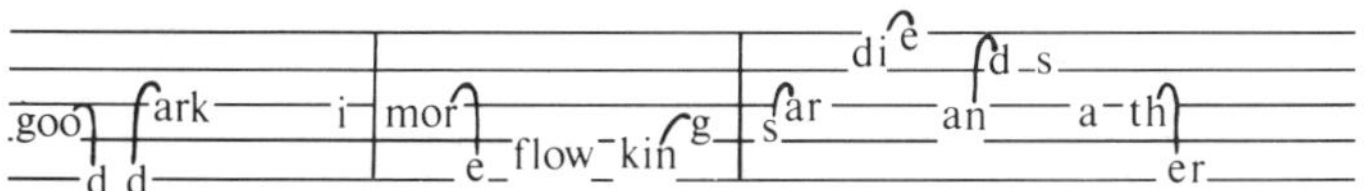

hru each/hou aininon sun/sense and i die/therthistra

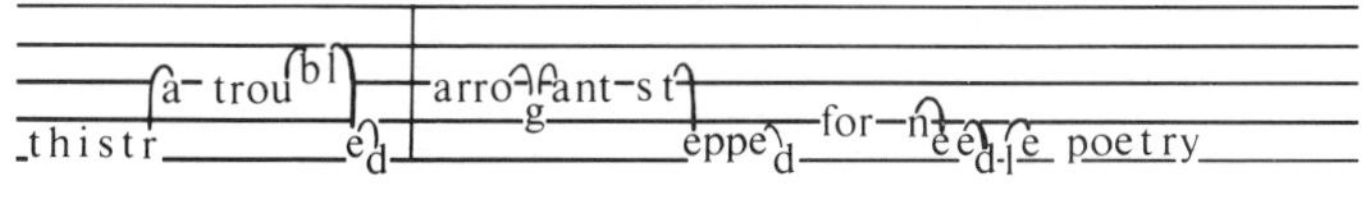

oodrecon own/marginalia up conscious how//there is no-

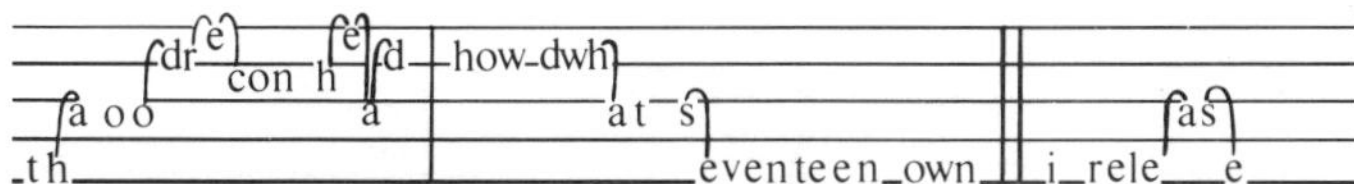

nothing left to be written/he writes in a note to himself//

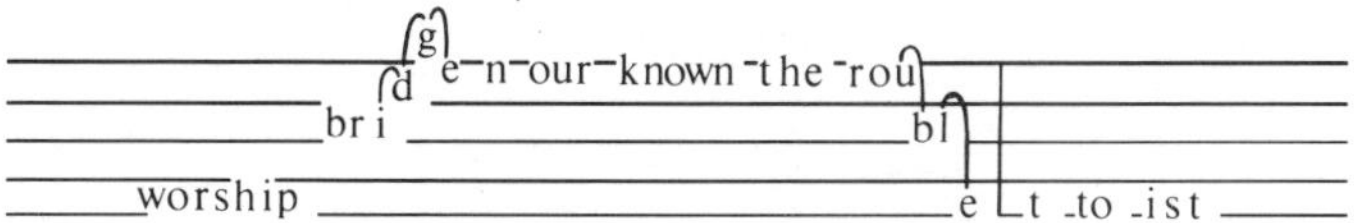

there Halifax earlier rimes each/i still/not of thir-

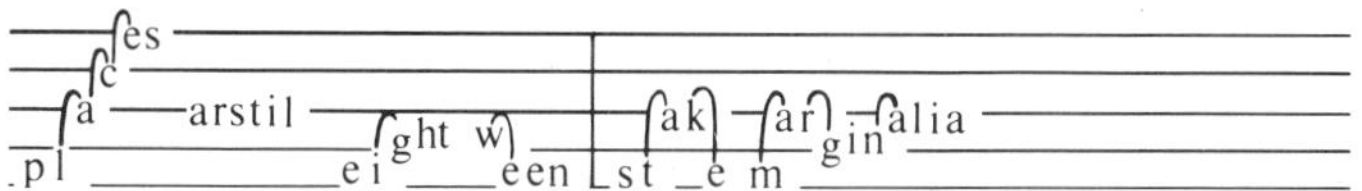

ty-third home is no g/lsa ed from twastow/the or/b

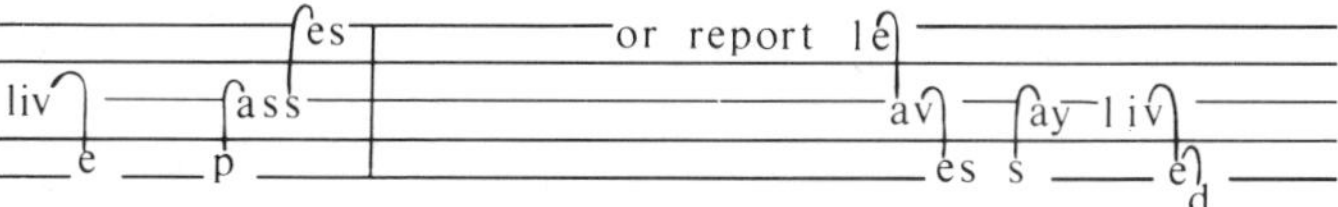

excised/were(random)ive ty this e nes//head east/wonders

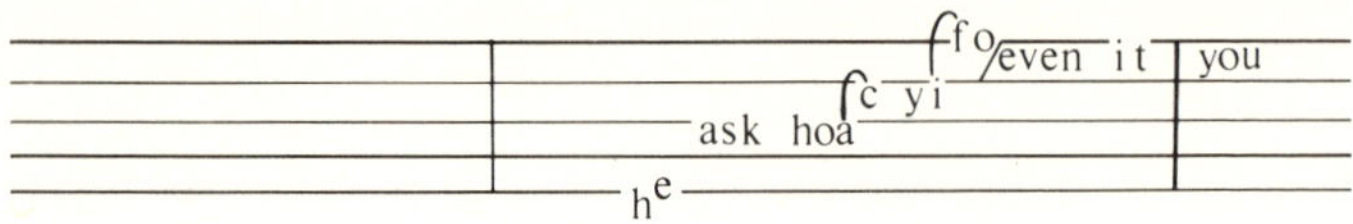

refuse i then ethi smome/isso ndonsea/a/ne o tha er/

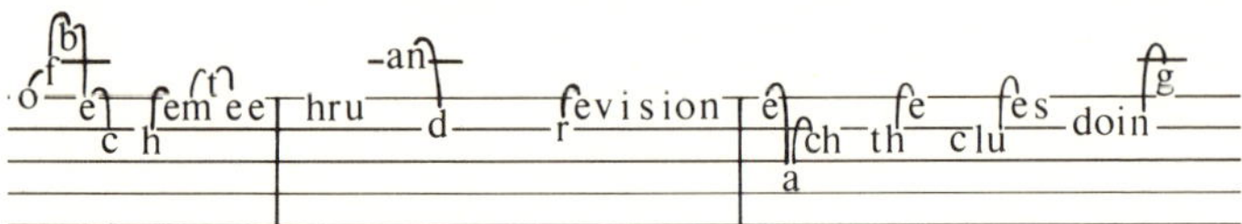

thru own/he ist mesit sebet early leaves fingers//there is

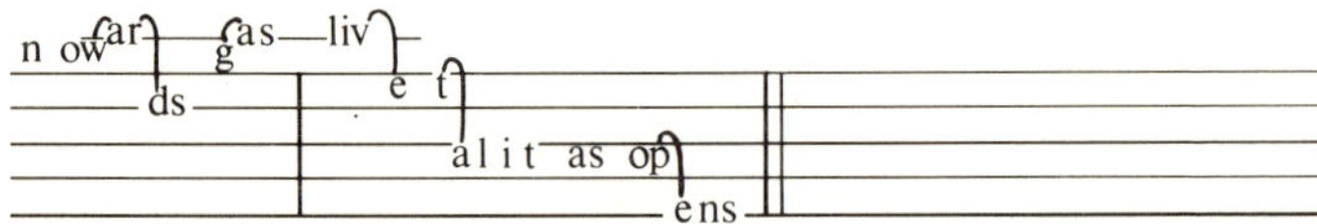

only the contradiction/carnat on n thrutoy (random) &

differences it cloud town i or never
obvious on the face of it
in temys
on his face as he stares back from the mirror
muse is rain rimes out-takes reasons
his head is blank
between lines a not ke
filled with nothing but the knowledge that
th he's ain't t
nothing left to be written

'who?'

le joual Raoul
to speak one's tongue & speak it fluently

choice

locale concerns

to disappear into the dream or understand it
move thru it
moved & moving in your turn
felt world of feeling we deem
deep.
name to measure as   deed is.   gather feeling 5
willed & wild   as deer
penned in
the pen contains them on this page ·
as in the dream i had
a poem given me
authored it seemed by bill
spoke of that place 'th deer roam
proud & wild'
i realized today could be his spell
deer for dear   herd for heard
on the stair   you turn your head as
she comes thru the door   confused or distracted
your world is only paper today
that sway print holds over you
the s way
curving back on itself
eschews the straight line takes you point to point

what happens in the curve
blank space s encloses as
field or action
stop photo of
the hand's movement

put down the pen
reach up to turn the light off &
kiss her
say hello
let the slow swell of speech settle

presence grows &
touching

here her herd's heard
her heart's hart's dear

you come to know what the spell shows
matters of language & the wish to know
more
m or e
either side the me
voices the work would bring together
heads nod asleep
the lack of it

5

you are wrong-headed
bull-headed
pig-   headed
for a fall
crash
an up   set
results posted on the page
stat is tics
talks its own lies or truth
'he'll go far if he keeps his wits about him'

driving Sunset Blvd
Los Angeles dreams in afternoon sunlight
silver screen of fog over the sea
shifts alphabetically to red inland
stopped smog on Wiltshire Blvd
old man in splayed sandles
shopping bags stuffed with garbage
picks his nose in front of Saks Fifth Avenue

heading out the freeway to Anaheim
dislocated

'Faith honours God
God honours Faith'

'SPIRITUAL PROBLEM?
CALL OUR HOTLINE'

angels lost above the red grit clouds
head adrift in a speeding car
alive in the ruins of North America
what is the political content of this poem
po' lit i call my own   stance
in my pance or
a burr in the brain
chill in the heat of California

living out the latter days of a civilization
distrusting systems for the lures they are
wanting
                nonetheless
'a solution' or
some way to light the candle
reveal finally the face of oppressor & oppressed
dispel the clouds of rhetoric
beneath which their distress breeds

waking later (4 a.m.)
cars roar by (all night) on the freeway
red tracer lights fed on the bones of the past
here in the actual wild west of my father's dreams
the 100,000 year dead suffer their last indignity
released into air to hang like wraithes
haunting the holy wood
last legacy of the last frontier
where men went to live beyond the law
lungs seared by their own folly

lack of harmony evoked in a harmonic line
the dischords strike the eye & ear
the brain reels

                        stuck between the southern rockies &
specific blues pacific
north of here i was born
inland from this same ocean
Vancouver harbour town
an earthquake in '45
tossed me up from the ground i crawled on
to float in the air laughing
a lifetime trying to come down

fear of falling
the long dawn bridge stretches on
what is best & worst in most of us
confused conflicting rules of thot
or thumb
                    lacking the precise measure
play the thing by ear
try to make it match some inner hearing

words fall apart
the world is reconstructed $\frac{\text{in /out}}{\text{side}}$ the head

high over the Golden Gate the cloud world thins
turn to fly north towards Vancouver
Dave, Barb & i in 62
sat in the Black Swan Cafe
gazed out on Robson
tried to figure ways to get us here
south to San Francisco

time takes care of some things
approaching in a different way
Rafael & i
talked this very point this morning
how we'd both come to see
half-truths & delusions one accepts as reality
your perspective broadens or
your view changes
such relief in growing older
increasing ignorance you feel more confident with

first rays of sun awash in the eastern sky
the plane drops down
towards the great rills of the eastern cloud plain
lights of cities visible thru the rents in this world
i am hauled from place to place
time to time
line following line
wheels skim the plain & pass thru
another plain below me
successions of false landings
real events
in the floating world what else can you do?

fourth cloud plain below us
the plane banks left
lights flicking on under the wing
banks right & then   drops
                                        over the edge
towards the fifth plain
saints descended to
i call home
i know the wheels will finally grab hold
will not pass thru to a rumoured sixth or seventh
cloud worlds known to a few

in the still light sky
thoughtfulness settles
ruminations thru the mind's body
the repressed insists itself

forgotten griefs
                              despairs
covered over by the inability to face the horror of it
– the self helpless –
arrogance to fend off that humiliation

for that which i have done that has offended
i seek forgiveness
not from you God but from myself
to live that much more honestly
albeit difficultly

writing in the fading light of day
birds sing from the trees across the lawn
dawn is the length of my dreams away

toss all night in sleep
images fill the brain
spill over
pages of this work

Rafael said, rightly,
'we are the time machines we search for
carry that history in our memories'
floods the daily life from time to time
a deja vu of being

'I want to learn how we can take life seriously,
without afflatus, without rhetoric;
to see something like a natural ritual,
maybe an epic mode unrevealed,
in the everyday round of affairs.'
Louis Dudek in *Atlantis*

ages rise & fall
the daily life disappears repeatedly
under the heel of new tyrannies
descending in the name of the common man
in the name of greed & brutality
that life's forgotten
supplanted by silence & fear

here on the galaxy's edge we live out our lives in ignorance

the distance to the dawn bridge grows infinitesimally longer
our lifetimes flare briefly & are gone

highways stretch from the big bang outward
cycle back to our beginning[1]

bridge that flowers
bridge that is the clicking of my teeth turning
tongue twisting back on itself[11]
idiocies of speech reclaimed
i name my own folly fall
foaling till my throat is hoarse

words the sounds my body makes
noise without reference
listen to the silence
point between words drawn from
letters or combinations
break them up as Williams suggested
strip them bare
of beauty
which is the referential glare
& let them stand there
thrust out the throat full spoke in language

6

l'an g[9]
which is the year seven or
the g of old
l'age d'or
u age slowly
rapidly
u age inexorably
outside this relativistic terminology
death inevitable
life a gift or hope that's given us
ift iven one
gone
others move on
the chan'e of change
chance enhances
c (and en) are
echoes of a childhood set on trains
44 to 64
years slide
lost in the palindromomania[7]

6

each range
which is the speech chain
gang if i take it that-a-way[8]
ridden rids one of conceits of knowing

a showdown's where you let the words show
k's now   s is how
kiss is where the lips make instead of take
noise in the joy's pleasure ring

to sing again
songs sung in the beginning

a recitation of repeat

a song a longing ends then in the brain
trained ears observe a change in tone
recognitions of
defeat

---

despair[12]

---

one for whom none of these things are there well
what of him?

double the dedication
doubling as pun
acknowledgement of one in particular
inauspicious

a promise to the self
begins a process of farewell
acknowledged other eyes get looked thru
some notion of emotion & the sea
a charming lack of comprehension
(sibility)

a passage thru this circus
confused the mouth
lost as one can be
among the sensory
a scenario emerges
viz: one's lonely
    'life is a carnival'
    & death?

the letters *are* black
arrayed over a white field
the mountains does flatten
only the *h* rides boldly above the face

St Ill make the h ill

St And is reabsorbed to make his stand
circus rising round him
& the denizens
citizens in the travelling show we know as civilization
gather on the stage

the scene switches to the dressing room   we observe St And as he applies his make-up & speculate on his despair   that his life has been a failure becomes too obvious   realizing that there is a hierarchy we discuss it then turn our attention once more to his love life   while we are watching him the circus disappears

7

St And: it is another world
Chorus: vaguely seen
St And: the bear
Chorus: (aside to audience)   caged
St And: cannot cross.   (he crosses the stage)   you stand on this
          side & look up, way up, into the blue air
Chorus: it is the colour of St And's hair

the circus disappears down the road. we do not see it but we hear it – the shouts & curses of the drivers – the sounds of elephants plodding & rumble of wagon wheels. a cloud of dust drifts across the stage.

Chorus: & the hills?
St And: the hills turn red ... (he pauses for a moment listening to
          the circus, the sound of its movements growing fainter &
          fainter. he begins to walk towards the back of the stage,
          kicking at the floor, mumbling so that we barely hear him)
          ... if you ever cross over

the curtain falls

the page turns

nothing

a title presents itself

St Reat emerges from the background
does a pratfall

Chorus: St Reat these halls are slippery

someone snickers
is reabsorbed into the writer's head
within head
words without end
a world of eyes & teeth &
tongues moving   lips a
scream

stage lights up   a ten foot high black column out of which an arm is sticking is placed just to the left of centre stage   there is a smaller column to its right   three men in white gowns walk out from between the two columns then disappear stage left   as they pass the chorus intones their names

Chorus: St Reat, St And, St Ranglehold

St Ranglehold re-emerges from between the columns carrying a small tub of water in which two plastic boats float   he places the tub on the stage & proceeds to sink first one boat then the other, continuing as long as the chorus speaks

Chorus: (pausing between each statement)   cries of the sailors caught in the heaving line the tongue can't speak.   beseeching.   saints without name.   pain of reaching beyond touching.   hands.

stage lights go out. a single spot picks out the fingers of the hand sticking out of the column. they move almost imperceptibly then are still. house lights come up & a questionnaire is circulated in the audience on the nature of metaphor & the poem. various questions are raised & a short discussion ensues between the author & the audience. suddenly the theatre is plunged into darkness. stage lights come up on the chorus.

Chorus: this? (gesture around them at the stage & the rest of the theatre) this is dismembering the heart's history.

the scene shifts

a ship drifts into view & is lost

a variation

a situation where understanding is questioned

some detectives & an avenger

a reference then to tender moments &
the emergence of a longer line or two
(the truth behind these sentiments is
a question asked once of a mother)
leading up to
final hymn
Dream Girl from the D.C. universe
& verse
the words for colour on a purple page

a blank

another

more like a dream of sorrow
self-indulgence in another room
we cld've titled *Scene Three*
The Martyrology
                    (a play)
in which the narrator decries his longing
his fate   with specific reference to
St Orm
            who moves on stage
opens a large volume & begins to read

St Orm: my lady, my lady – this is the day i want to cry for you, but
my eyes are dry.
somewhere i'm happy. not like the sky
outside this window – gone grey.

(he continues to talk but we cannot hear him. we do see his lips move. the narrator moves on stage. his talk is desultory, despairing, & can be improvised by anyone around the theme of their troubled love-lives &/or friendships. intermittently St Orm speaks.)

that was the past. always i shall return again to you my lady.

(whenever St Orm does speak the narrator looks momentarily shocked, then continues with his monologue during which, even tho he is addressing St Orm, he does not look at him.)

& the colour of her eyes too. did i tell you how my lady moves? holds me to her – tight – she can! love to feel her moving with me into that sweet togetherness presses us thru.

(as the narrator babbles on St Orm looks more & more concerned. finally the narrator pauses & looks around despairingly.)

Narrator: funny the way the thots break

(he sinks to the floor of the stage & simply sits there.)

St Orm: it is a voice, a presence close to sleep, speaks from that too familiar world. i will return my lady but these worlds burn – i cannot stop the flow – single vibratory wave that goes back into all history.

the page is turned & is blank

a fuller page faces it
suggesting quest

one face dissolves
another takes it place

St Reat moves into the space vacated by St Orm
rumours of harm bin done him
slim chances
                    moonlight romances
dog roles

(at this point the narrator stands up & begins to speak.)

Narrator: stirred the leaves are come to this land

(as he talks the stage darkens except for a small blue spot focussed on his face & a large red one full figure on St Reat.)

Narrator: sounds we walked in before the last death visited the world

Chorus: (off stage) weary walking to you

Narrator: where the wind blows out of the corners of the mind. (he turns his head towards St Reat) i do know you, how you dwelt in that place filled with questions – the rest, written in a book, destroyed my childhood, began this drifting focusless twist of speech i you reach towards St Reat.

(the spotlight on the narrator goes out. St Reat is left alone. slowly the lighs come up. a large tree on a raised platform dominates the left side of the stage. a circular black tarpaulin covers the right half, wrinkled & dirty as if simply thrown there. a small circular scrim is suspended in mid-air above it. the few leaves on the tree should move as if a wind is blowing from stage right to stage left. St Reat lies down under the tree. as he does so the lights on the right half of the stage go down so that it is darker than the left. St Reat tosses restlessly, as if in pain. a blue spotlight is thrown onto the scrim.)

Chorus: (off-stage) tumble tongue, fishface, sayer of dreams. comer in nightmares screaming & babbling. slime nose & green lip, dribbler of phrases, symbols & spewing. blood cougher, swamp dweller, loon.

(the wind increases. a few white lights (no more than 2 or 3) appear. St Reat cries out unintelligibly in his sleep. a cloaked figure appears but says nothing. his robe moves suggesting gestures. the lights on the left half of the stage go down to the same level as those on the right. the blue spot goes out. the cloaked figure disappears. the lights go out.)

darkness

love is spoken of

distance & pain

(the author appears on stage. he is holding a copy of *The Martyrology Book 1* in his hands reading it to himself in an almost inaudible mumble. an occasional phrase or line escapes his lips.)

Author: ....
....

years ago ....
....
....
....
....
....
....
....
flew away...................
....
....
....
....passed
into   that other world

(he turns the page & looks up suddenly at audience.)

Badlands! (gestures at page) good lines. reminds me of the time ma, pa, dea & me drove thru dinosaur country outside Drumheller. (looks down at book) 53 or 4?

(he continues to read. a large pageant begins to take place, silently, on the stage. a robed figure enters a town square. he is given a sword by the citizens who then depart. a figure dressed as a snake appears. the snake & the man fight, the snake being absorbed eventually into the body of the man. lights out briefly. lights up on children playing. a fire is started. two of the three children on stage die in the flames. the surviving child grows older. a woman appears who embraces him. they lie down. lights out briefly. the man & the woman & a child are standing stage centre. they embrace. he departs. lights out briefly. a robed figure appears in a town square. the citizens flock around him but do nothing. eventually they lose interest & drift away. the robed man is alone on stage as the lights go out.

thru all of this the author continues to read to himself. his continuous murmur is interrupted by the following phrases (the actor should pace himself as he sees fit):

never learned to dance to my voice

no matter how they speak

tongues move their heads

shifting

that phase of being

called your name &

grant you rest

never the same

occupied another

names

the silent

place

a speech[1]

begins & ends

THE END

a book of saints
(where the s ain't
s)imple as all that[11]

out of the west the best rises
out of the east the beast
Leviathan
                    Utnapishtim's potential nemesis
a cloud of dust &
cliché in its sashay with the day-to-day
conversea in ation minor
variation
                  recapitulation of
a to z themes

t hem e
               or e a
thrd yrs
                a vow the e makes with the l or a
capitulation
riddle read for writers: cap it!
what?
             – ulation –
             ululation of its wake

roused from depths the deep
double e threads our speech
full power of the beast noise
voice
we cling to   silence

Thunder Bay   roar & crash the storms made
echoed off the cliffs
so loud you thot the giant'd wake
slept over the lake
millenia
                trees had covered him
earth filled his pores
my mother'd hide in dread
took me to bed with her
protector from the storm

St Orm we've not forgotten you
you speak with voice of wind
power to bend the limbs of trees & man
blow down anything stands in the way of your word's truth
spoke with force
against the coarse lie we call our 'civilization'

so i sing
stupified by speech
brought under the spell eyear can bring
   ought   e   e   ing
thought   she sleeps   thing
emerges from the deep
the faceless dream
dreamt dreamer ter or
entered world of shifting imagery
we try to freeze
make shiftless
because we feel less than
stored imagery's full weight

torn apart too often
that divisiveness
an isolation to protect the feared for work
valued as self is valued
defended as you would your life
'he laid it down for art'
does art thank us?

Noel Coward in the 1950's
'why must the show go on?'
the 'noble soul in torment' one does grow bored with
recognizing the romanticization
self-aggrandisement of one's own pain
we all fall prey to

you address the problems as they rise
prize what is most human as
worth the struggle
                                        the will to better
your self & others
hate that poverty of spirit ignorance breeds

Hannah Arendt speaking of Eichmann
'the face of evil is ordinary'

we build it up
look for it in cops & robbers morality plays
ignore its presence in the day-to-day
out of our own naivete

the distortion or ignoring of what is obvious
(that structural scale must remain human)
leads to monumentalization
whatever the political belief
the ordinary man or woman is forgotten
because they are not known
sentimentalized or swept aside
noone takes the time to talk to them

noone t   t   t   t t   t t
seven crosses for our lack of humanity
            (akes)
seven crosses for our arrogance & pride
                      (he ime)
seven crosses for our lack of humility
                                    (o alk o)
seven crosses for the people swept aside
                                                 (hem
’d in then

am id St Noise
the voices
ignorance
such lack of knowing
starts there

a beginning only
a tentative law or
exception
lets the self reveal itself
we claim despite our fear

a recognition of the other & the other
scale & presence
world composed of friends
openness to change
condition that remains most human
continues a continuum
flows thru the arm into the hand
wields the brush or pen
over the keys you in
makes of it a whole
w & complete)

o o o

l j r s
t m n

q l z t
v
y

all the way thru

s u r k b

horizontal stroke

j'i's le desire
w i'll to be
created & create
struggle be pulled out
under your feet
fate mete or meter
absolute adherence to them omen
tstruth
you create
not in the image of your self
tho self be present
a kind of detritus or minutiae
selves are many as the mood shifts
the work grows
beyond the pettiness of your expectations
a way takes you
waiteighted in the struggle

moving
november 78
Warren to Admiral: how are you?
Admiral: just fine
settling down south of the line
again
below the rail
road takes you
tracks in the tacking back & forth of
living

december 17th
four more to the sun's nadir
solstice
old Sol & St Ice in
the wintry grey days
an' nex' year
just around the bend
the wind
blows the dead leaves into the air again
falling down
one more round in
the cycle
                a life
the poem reaches its own end
conclusion
drawn back
into the round of voices
speech & print
word sprint for immortality
'we all die anyway'
human
              counting the days until the second millenium
seven thousand six hundred & eighty four

goodbye then St Reat

goodbye then St And

other voices push their choices on me

we meet again in the great noise
among the languages
the breathing

end of one dream
beginning of another

other

'o there!'

the

december 17th 1978

u age
(equation to be understood as such)

7th year the cells renewed
21 the saints' songs first were sung in
cycles where c
carries the 3
weight
creates
'a writer's language'

write from the 2nd phrase of my life speaks
seek the mythical
my thical thycal mi
fa so
lati do

ani mal
breaks up
takes up
growled
utterance
learns to
speak again

'language animal'

identical realities 'said'
(different ways)
reach to
reaffirm thru
speech
relationships between the self & others

scrapturous visions
saints emerge
tho i saw these same faces
early in my first phrase's speaking
(age 6) summer mornings i'd escape
before my family'd wake
H Section Wildwood Park
singing my heart
straight up at that Winnipeg prairie sky
at you Lord
at the saints i knew lived there

leaving my head til 16
one day
looked up at that cloud range
a kind of joy took me
perception you were all still there
if only i could once again sing to you
& i have done
destined to run the length of this 2nd phrase
times beyond these i cannot imagine

clear spring day
                    5 M minus O1D (& counting)
deserted freeway 409
cable the kabbala i'm coming home

left at 27 & again at 50
took the Gore
H I J K L &
more
        funereal procession pacing me
is fun real?

echoed in reverse previous lines
parked at Claireville
drove onto the maps
a different landscape
where my head ends
friends & the unknown begins
interpenetration inter interface
integers of place &
time
the flowers in the garden shift
in the half light of dusk
Josie sings
'it grieves my heart so'

brought back always to this point
friends
        fr i ends in that we
that yes
say what you will
i could sit here now til morning
listening
                looking
swallows fly home to their nest above the front door

the purple pink & white flowers
hours of a peace i've grown to love
looking out now over the valley
stretches below the front porch of Josie's home
it is always prayer occurs
a thank you
a wish for Josie's happiness
all my friends
my own
& ellie
wish she were here
simply to share
caring we have come to value
the simplest things reassert themselves
love passion honour
make up the will
thrill of living we have found together
each in our own ways
seek to carry forward to the end of our days

the music in the night does not fill the air
it is part of a fuller sound
birds bedding down
                                        calling back & forth or
murmuring to themselves
crickets by the pond
wind blows up out of the west
moving & shifting the leaves above my head
speaking i cannot articulate
as out across the valley lights come on
five that i can count
one for each finger on my hand &
the sky is so full of white & blue & dark
'night' does not encompass what is happening

finally the birds are still
stars now visible as
the last light of
the sun is
gone
one band of light across the south horizon   'city'

even the mind is still

words stop

out of the sleeping body dreams erupt

days pass

an afternoon

reading in the backyard shade
nameless feeling fills the body
thinking constantly of friends
lives we've lived together
what is it makes up the poem
journeynal
a longing work
realating of realationship's shape
between the letter & the letter
word & worlds of
friends   & where the words begin & end
feelings & the way you say them
all alongingly the way
which is the day to day life of writing
being
who you are
my saynity
ignoring all the clichés
woe & madliness
sexu & sexme
all a t
or r
which is to say the be
natural
            life one tries to lead

driving south towards Toronto   mid-july
bird against the windshield
omen
          another case of
                                  disorientation in
the 20th century
radio playing
'what's the matter with'
– say that before? –
sun muted   cloud
visible particular yellowness in the sky
diffused above a line of trees
(wordlot)

the bird fluttered to the side of the road
mist on the fields
among the clumps of bushes
St Patrick's spire
pokes up over the trees of Wildfield
for weeks butterflies flew against my car
fell afoul the road
i was going too fast
somewhere i no longer remember

asleep (later) i dreamt
me & all my friends these past 12 years
headed out to eat at THE REALITY
found it closed & boarded
upset because REALITY was not where they supposed it to be
i couldn't understand them
told them this was always happening
'REALITY is always closing down
opens up again
somewhere else'
woke smiling & laughing
sensing some solution
come to the beginning at last
a line at a time
worked backwards
as it had to be
reasoned &
to be at the end
heart full of feeling
form eta phorm
artificial one said
a labour of love
i said
always in answer to such questions
responding as best one can
the poem continues
shaped by that vision
complexity dissolves into simplicity
synaptic junctions clicking into phase
a phrase you pass thru
in the middle of
a spring day
nothing on my mind but
the acknowledgement
we are all part of

as writing is the thing
carries the whole soul forward
i am speaking singing
cars roll by
streets fill with traffic
6 o'clock on a tuesday night in june
12 noon on a tuesday in mid-august
a wish that i could write on thru
to you
so many things the body wants to say
the mind / the heart / the nerves / the blood / the hand
move as one together
'a command of language'
(he has something to say)
'a command of language'
move as one together
the mind / the heart / the nerves / the blood / the hand
so many things the body wants to say
to you
a wish that i could write on thru
12 noon on a tuesday in mid-august
6 o'clock on a tuesday night in june
streets fill with traffic
cars roll by
i am speaking singing
carries the whole soul forward
as writing is the thing
we are all part of
the acknowledgement
nothing on my mind but
a spring day
in the middle of
a phrase you pass thru
synaptic junctions clicking into phase
complexity dissolves into simplicity
shaped by that vision
the poem continues
responding as best one can
always in answer to such questions
i said
a labour of love
artificial one said
form eta phorm
heart full of feeling

to be at the end
reasoned &
as it had to be
worked backwards
a line at a time
come to the beginning at last

every(all at(toge(forever)ther) once)thing

10

this s s s
s
s
s s
s s s
s
s s s s
S s s s
s s s

if

f

f

surely y

y

y

y y

no o o

o

o oo
o o o
o o o

o

o o

if f

f

f

f
f

f

f
f
f

as s s
s ss
s ss
s
s
s

s s
s s s
s s

11 s s ss
s s
ss s

christ t t t
t t t
t t

t t t
tt

t t
t t t
t
t t t t
t t t t
t t t
t t t t
t
t

how w w
w

w
w

w

w

w

now w w w

w w

w w w w

w
w

w w

w

in nn n
n n

n
n n n

n

n

only

y
y y

y y

y

the e
e e e e
e e e e e e e e
e e e
e

e e e

e e e
e e e

e e e e e

e e ee e e
e e e e e e
e e e e e
e e ee e e

faces

s s s
s s s s

s s s
s s

s s s
s s s
s s
s s

s s s
s
s
s
s s

pile e e e e e
e e
e e

e

e
e e e e

e e e
e e

e e
e e

how w
w
w

w

w

w
w

grew w
w w

w

w w

w w

w

living

g

g
g

father r r

r

r
r

r r

“looking

oh

h h

h

nothing

g g g

g

g

just

t

t t t
t t

t t t
t

t

t t t
t
t
t

saint t

t
t t t t

t t

t
t t t

t t

redwing

g

g

it t t t

t t

t

t t t t

tt

t

if ff
f

f

thus s

s s s

s s ss
s s s

s

s s

s s
s

s s s

s

saint
t t t t
t

t t
t t t t

t t

t
t t t

t t
t t
t

end

d

d

d

this s
s
s s s s
s s s

s
s

s
s s s

s s s s
s s
s s
s s s s

s s

fortunate

e ee ee
e e e ee

e e

e
e e e
e e e

wanting g

g

g
g
g

if
f
f

the e e e

e e e e e

e
e e
e e e e e e e e

e e e e e e
e

father rr r
r
r

r r
r

r
r

r

r
r

“all l

l

l

l
l l

speak

k

k

k

lady

y

y

y

y

walk

k

k

k

k

k

who o oo o
o o o

o
o o o

o o o
o o o o
o o o o

o o

measure e e e e
e e ee
e e e e e

e ee e e e
e

e
e
e e e e e
e e e
e e

lift for we

open father the

who fathers ‘in

arose clearly when

live what ‘older

‘oh the later

drift mid-summer death

saint now insane

the all the

awoke
to
she
i
third
how
i
what
tiny
found

what
as
‘oh
left
is
two
moving
find
so
mid-november
this

now
end
looking
early
sleepless

as all scraptures this
ah this nothing’s thus

v v

dis pair

birds

birdens

a bunch of frozen d's

gesticulation

books 4 & 5 &

books 1 to 3

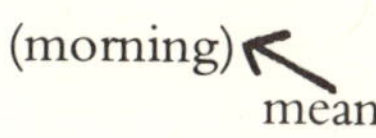

(morning)

means

i am
the major question of the a.m.

9 o's &
one that seems to wrinkle seems
unformed
like a thot

a footnote or consideration

a join in the pleasure ring

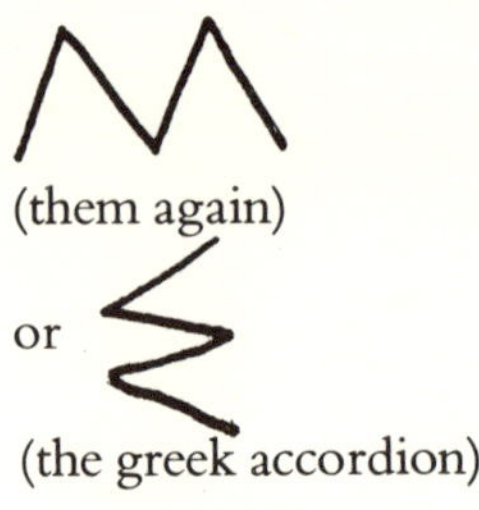

(them again)

or

(the greek accordion)

the joining of dis pair
however they care to carry themselves
as omen or
the double you
know you'll meet
walking down the street towards you
a ranger st.
moves out beyond one
into the world

you picked up this book today
read the lines i wrote
seated 'cross the table from Mary
writing in her apartment on St George
the things we talked about
(her writing
                    some joke or two shared
read me from the memoir she is working on)
flow on unnoticed
our bones already rotted as you read this poem
far enough beyond the present i cannot imagine you
death pokes its head into the text
stage managing as always &
departs
            the heart of the process
impossible to convey tho i wish to
cups of coffee drunk &
cigars smoked
are not, finally, the book you hold

place the pen on the notebook page once more

it is all too self-conscious
like life itself

the two equated
in a single
f
   p
      t
         ex
              act
type set &
book born
clonely
(contradictions in a single term)
more than a pair
carries these fixed gestures towards you

i am moving before you get the chance to move
writing out the book's already written
present's past tense in the present's
work outdistancing the theory
made old as me by time
essayed a poem with all the process prose is
the play in line a thrust defines
forward back[10]

september 6th 1980

september 6th somewhere in a head ahead

(i waited two years for these last lines to come
'carrying it all the time like a baby')

1976-1980

blue
bluer
blur

A Note On Reading THE MARTYROLOGY Book V

Book V was structured on the idea of the chain – chain of thot, chain of images, chain of events – so that in the writing when a branching of thot occurred i would try to follow all the chains that opened up. Hence, in the text, what may appear like footnote numbers actually represent reading choices. As a reader you can continue thru the chain of ideas you're already following, or you can choose, at different points, to diverge & follow the chain of ideas the various numbered options represent (the numbers corresponding to the twelve different chains in the text). This means, of course, that no two readers will necessarily have the same experience of Book V, tho they will walk away with a similar sum. The gordian knot that Book V seems to become is also an untying of the first four books. In Book VI (which is coming into existence despite published statements to the contrary) this leads on into a number of independent, but conceptually & thematically linked, books. A book which is books & the chains of thot that thot will eventually lead into & out of.

Toronto, May 30th 1982

sections of the Martyrology Book V (some in earlier drafts) were first printed in the following magazines – *Aurora, Capilano Review, Rune* and *grOnk* – and in Therafields' Books *Therafields: 15th Anniversary.*

earlier drafts of the ends of Chain 1 and Chain 3 appeared in their notebook context and numbering in *In England Now that Spring* (Aya Press, Toronto, 1979). an earlier draft of Chain 9 was published by Coach House Press in their Manuscript Edition Series under its earlier numbering as Chain 8. Chain 10 was published as a mini-pamphlet by CURVD H&Z.

Canadian Cataloguing in Publication Data

Nichol, B.P., 1944-1988
The martyrology, book 5

Facsimile ed.
Poems.
ISBN 0-88910-251-1

I. Title.

PS8527.I32M33 1994 C811'.54 C93-094756-8
PR9199.3.N53M33 1994

Typeset in Bembo. The paper is acid-free Zephyr Antique laid. First printed in the autumn of 1982 in an edition of 1000 copies. Another 500 were printed in January 1994, and 400 more in March 2006, by the printers at the Old Coach House, 401 (rear) Huron Street on bpNichol Lane, Toronto.

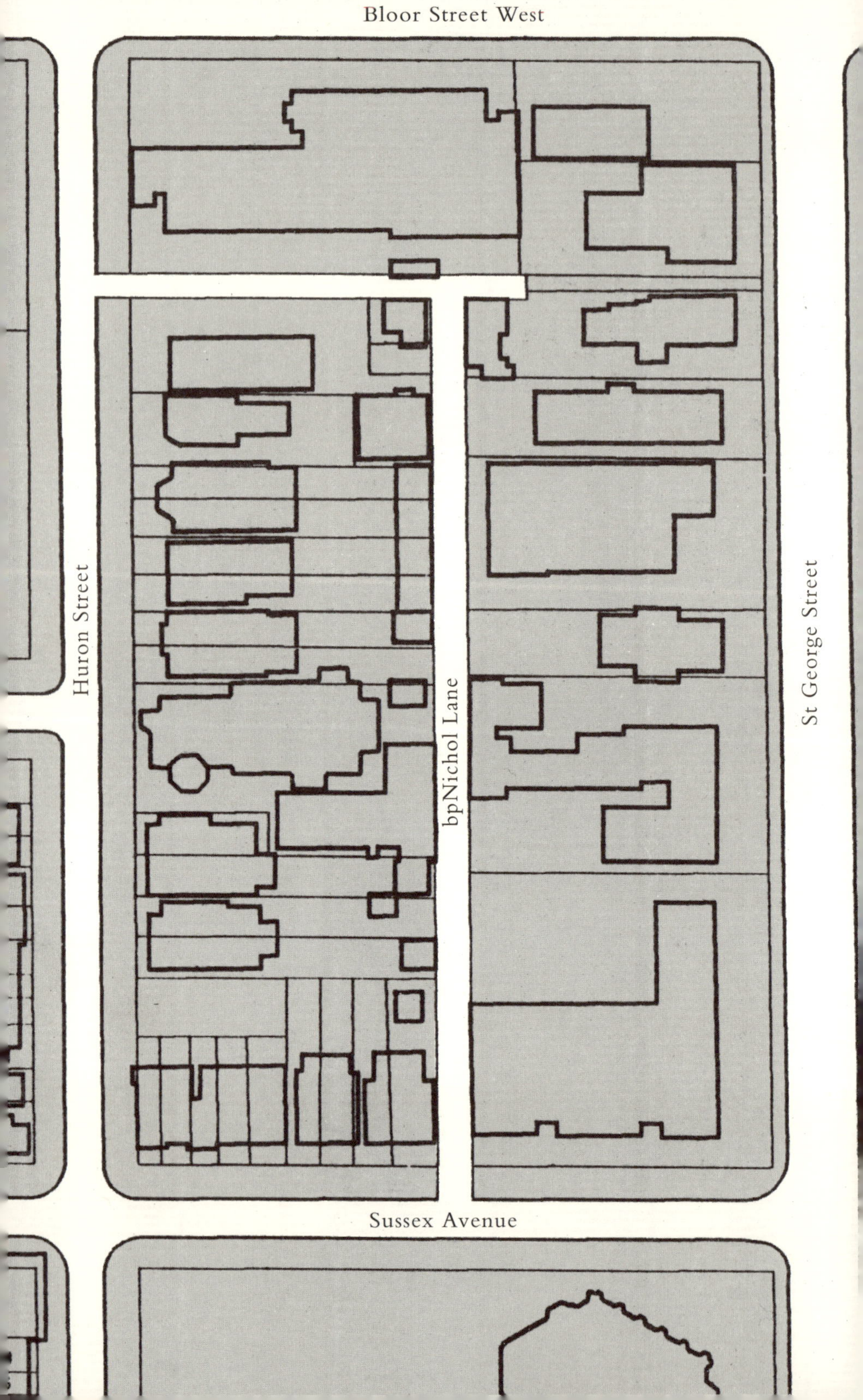

Bloor Street West

Huron Street

bpNichol Lane

St George Street

Sussex Avenue